The Snake Prince
and Other Stories

The Snake Prince

and Other Stories

Burmese Folk Tales

Collected and retold
by Edna Ledgard

INTERLINK BOOKS
An imprint of Interlink Publishing Group, Inc.
NEW YORK

First published 2000 by

INTERLINK BOOKS
An imprint of Interlink Publishing Group, Inc.
99 Seventh Avenue • Brooklyn, New York 11215 and
46 Crosby Street • Northampton, Massachusetts 01060
www.interlinkbooks.com

Library of Congress Cataloging-in-Publication Data

Ledgard, Edna.
    The snake prince and other stories : Burmese folk tales /
collected and retold by Edna Ledgard.
        p.   cm.
    ISBN 1-56656-313-5 (paperback)
1. Tales--Burma.   I. Title.
    GR309.L44   1999
    398.2'09591--dc21   99-30328
                                               CIP

Printed and bound in Canada
10 9 8 7 6 5 4 3 2 1

To request our complete catalog,
please visit our website: www.interlinkbooks.com,
call us at 1-800-238-LINK or write to:
Interlink Publishing
46 Crosby Street, Northampton, MA 01060
e-mail: info@interlinkbooks.com

Contents

Acknowledgments

Many people have made this work possible but some are so special and pivotal that they must be named! Therefore, my special thanks to Daw Saw Yi of the Burma Baptist Convention in Rangoon, Burma (Yangon, Myanmar). She has given many years of friendship and continued effort in advising, finding, and translating material for this work. Her associates, especially Than Than Htay, U Thong Tun, Thong Aye and others have helped search out and translate material for this book. Dr. Sein Lin and his wife Constance have also helped in translations and given their general encouragement.

Dr. Fred Dickinson (whom I knew as "Uncle Dickie") and his wife, Bertha, added to my knowledge of and checked my accuracy in naming trees, flowers, and animals. Dr. Irene Jones, a dear family friend, read one of my earliest adaptations and encouraged me to continue. Dr. Raymond Beaver, Alice M. Findlay, and Patricia Magdamo, all of ABC International Ministries, Valley Forge Pennsylvania, sent material and/or directed me to further useful sources.

My colleagues in the "Wednesday Writers" have encouraged me and offered excellent suggestions. My thanks to all, with particular thanks to Susan Aller, Barbara Barrett, Joan Horton, Joyce Stengel, Pegi Deitz Shea, and Laura Williams. And special thanks to Helen Hyman, who taught me and set my feet "on the path," and to Gertrude R. Russell who encouraged my early efforts.

In addition, permission to adapt was generously granted

by the following:

Oxford University Press, UK and India, and AMS Press, USA, for stories from *Burmese Folktales*, collected and translated into English by Dr. Maung Hting Aung;
AMS Press for stories from *The Glass Palace Chronicles*, translated into English by Pe Maung Tin and G.H. Luce;
Scholastic, Inc. for stories from *A Kingdom Lost for a Drop of Honey*, by Helen Trager and Dr. Mong Hting Aung;
S.C.M. Press, Ltd. for stories from *Told to Burmese Children*, collected and adapted by Maurice Russell;
Simon & Schuster for *Jataka Tales* and *More Jataka Tales* retold by Ellen C. Babbitt;
Dharma Publishing for assurance that all Jataka Tales are in the public domain.

Last, but most important, grateful thanks to my parents, Herbert E. Hinton and Marion Beekley Hinton for my life, my childhood experiences, the myths, fairy tales, Bible stories, and many other books they read to me and encouraged me to read; to those beloved "pests," my sister and brothers; to my Burmese "Aunties," Alice Thayer, Eva Cummins, Lucy Wyatt, and especially Marion "Auntie" Reifsneider; to my teachers and schoolmates at Taunggyi; and in a way, everyone who touched my life, particularly my early life in Burma.

My thanks, too, to my husband, children, and grandchildren who have cheered me on and to whom this book is dedicated.

All of these people have encouraged my interest in and respect for the many ways humankind struggles to see the universe and our place in it.

Preface

In 1935 I stood, at the age of eight, in a magnificent room of King Mindon's great palace at Mandalay. It was not my first visit nor quite my last, but it turned out to be the center of a web of events leading to this book.

The palace was not ancient, only about seventy-five years old, and there was no Burmese king to rule. For the previous fifty years, Burma had been British, and the British army occupied a substantial portion of the palace grounds. But some governor with good sense had insisted the significant buildings be set aside as a museum. It was truly an impressive sight. Visitors from all over the world remarked on it.

All the palace buildings were built entirely of teakwood. Sturdy fat pillars lofted extremely high ceilings. Clerestory windows let in dim light and refreshed the air. High threshold boards at every doorway discouraged easy access to rodents or snakes. Every inch of wall was carved into intricate scrolls of leaves, flowers, and various creatures, but the room I had just entered was unique. Tiny pieces of mirrored glass encrusted the entire room. Some brilliantly colored bits resembled rubies, emeralds, or sapphires, but most shone a clear diamond white. In that special room, brothers, sisters, and everything real simply vanished. Instead, Arabian princesses, neiblungs, *nagas*, unicorns, *chinthe*, and dancing *nats* surrounded me, echoing of the fabulous and fantastic. Yet the room was not fable.

With my fingers I could trace the leaves and flowers engraved into the warm teakwood. I could touch the cool glass jewels which were not jewels. This had been the antechamber

1

to King Mindon's great "Lion" throne room. Here ministers and envoys once waited for an audience with the king. Just over a hundred years earlier, King Bagyidaw, Mindon's uncle, gathered the best scholars, abbots, and court historians of the land at his own palace at Ava. He gave them his antechamber—his "glass palace room"—as a workroom, charging them with the formidable task of compiling an authoritative history of Burma. They were to examine all available written and oral records of that history, checking inscriptions found in pagodas and other monuments.

They selected and recorded the most consistent possible choices of dates, history, and legend they could find. (Incidentally, the English translation of their work reads as if the translator had learned English by reading the King James Bible.) The new document, called *The Glass Palace Chronicles of the Kings of Burma* in honor of the magnificent room where they worked, was completed in 1829, 106 years before I stood in the "Glass Palace Room" of King Mindon's palace. However, at eight, I was not yet aware of, nor particularly interested in such writings. And besides, seventy, eighty, or a hundred years might as well have been infinity to me then.

The palace reflected Brahmin-Buddhist cosmology, a world view that more than once interfered with a king's good judgment in dealing with the outside world! The imposing king's house, its seven-tiered golden roof soaring skyward, stood exactly in the center. It represented fabled Mount Meru (Myinmo Taung) with its seven ranges of hills. The golden and jeweled "Lion Throne" sat directly under the pinnacle of the tower. Here, it was believed, all the wisdom of the universe funneled down to guide the king as he sat, canopied beneath the white umbrella of kingship at the exact center of the palace-city.

The four queen's houses stood at each of the four cardinal points, representing the four great islands around Mount Meru. These, too, were ornately carved and decorated teak buildings, each with a throne room, each with private walled gardens and bathing pools. Lesser queens, concubines, ministers, abbots, and all manner of servants had been housed in various buildings in the palace-city. There had been fine stables for horses and magnificent stables for the royal elephants. The entire palace city was enclosed in a crenelated brick wall forming a perfect square, a little over a mile on a side. The walls precisely faced the four cardinal directions and were punctuated by twelve city gates, three on a side, each dedicated to a particular sign of the zodiac. Multi-tiered guard towers stood at each gate. Bridges led across the surrounding moat, which was filled with golden carp and sacred lotus.

The home of a missionary-teacher friend sat across the dusty road from the moat and those walls. I loved to visit her. We would make Valentines and birthday cards and paper crowns. But often we just sat, drinking in the muted blue-greens of the peaceful moat, the soft brick-red of the walls and the scarlet exuberance of the flame trees in bloom.

To the north of the palace, Mandalay Hill, sacred for thousands of years, rose like an earthen breast above the wide flat flood plain of the Irrawaddy. Indeed, Mindon had built his palace city to fulfill a prophesy. Tradition held that Gautama Buddha himself, with his disciple Ananda, had once walked on that hill. He had pointed to the south, and prophesied that on the 2,400th anniversary of his death, a "Golden City" would stand at its base. The anniversary year was 1857, and Mindon planned to fulfill the prophesy. Before the first stone was laid, Mindon erected a unique golden image of the Buddha standing on the sacred mount, pointing toward the city-to-be.

Then the flurry of building began. Soothsayers and astrologers were consulted to determine the propitious day for each task. Sacred rites of human sacrifice provided ghost warriors to guard the palace gates and buildings. At last, in 1861, while the Americans were fighting a bitter civil war, King Mindon moved his court into the newly completed palace-city at Mandalay. Today, as in 1935, Mandalay Hill is webbed with canopied stairways connecting the pagodas, images and holy shrines that speckle its sides. Fierce *chinthe*, those mythical crested lion dogs, guard the paths, reminding pilgrims to remove footwear before treading on holy ground. But most astonishing of all is the Kuthodaw at its base. A visitor might easily imagine he is in some nursery or spawning ground for infant pagodas. Within a high-walled enclosure, 729 small white pagodas cluster around a handsome white and gold "parent."

This cluster of pagodas, sometimes called "the world's largest book,"contains the entire *Tripitaka* (three baskets) of Buddhist sacred writings. Mindon had these writings carved onto marble tablets, enshrining each in its own small pagoda. Here, at last, were the sacred writings for all to read. In Mindon's time, the everyday city of Mandalay outside the palace walls was filled with the homes and shops of silversmiths, gold leaf beaters, lacquer workers, wood, pearl, and ivory carvers. All the artisans, fishermen, rice farmers, goat herders and common folk that were needed by a royal court filled the outer city or nearby villages. This had only slightly changed by 1935. Streets were still beds of dust, filled with horse carriages and bullock carts, wandering goats or half wild dogs, and a handful of cars, one of which was proudly owned by my father.

Our family lived in a brick building enclosed in a large compound and surrounded by a high brick wall with pieces of broken glass along the top to discourage thieves. This was Kelly High School, where Dad was superintendent, or *Sayagyi*. Privileged young Burmese men, most of whom were boarders, came to Kelly to learn the English, math, and science they would need to attend university in Rangoon or Oxford, England. Dad was also a missionary, but a Burman minister was the pastor and did most of the preaching at the small Baptist church next to the school.

A few blocks away, behind more high brick walls, stood a mission school for girls, run by three American women. We called them "Auntie" in the polite Burmese way, and they and the other teacher friend I mentioned were our "family" away from home. We were the only American children in the city and played mostly with our cook's Indian family. While we were small, we had an "Amah," a young Karen woman who watched us play, took us to the market, and slept on a cot in my bedroom. She told me Burmese folk tales as well as sometimes reading to me from the American books our Grandmother sent from Ohio. This freed Mother to participate in Dad's work.

Our visit to the palace probably occurred soon after Christmas, when my older brother and sister and I were all home on our long school vacation. For nine months of each year we lived in Taunggyi at The American School with two American teachers and about thirty children from American Baptist missions all over Burma. The school term ran from late February to early November, keeping us children in the healthy air of the cool Shan mountains during Burma's hot season. Sweltering heat in lowland stations such as Mandalay

5

added serious health risks to those of sanitation and diet. And we three were both jealous of and sorry for our little brother, who was allowed to be home with our parents, but was pink as a peony from prickly heat.

The mountain itself was intensely beautiful—misty blue valleys, forests of semi-tropical trees, stands of bamboo, fields of grasses and dry rice culture, and a constant breeze. We visited lakes and caves, and walked before breakfast each day up a wooded path. My three classmates and I spent many afternoons catching polywogs in a stream that ran by one edge of the property, or sitting in a large treehouse someone had built. We tilled vegetable gardens for the lessons of the earth and the fruits of our labors. And we weeded rose gardens as one of our punishments for forgetting rules. Those rules were more than strict: they were rigid, yet we had enough space and time both to enjoy the comradeship of our school "family" and to create quiet coves of solitude. It would take volumes to record all the pieces of memory from those first nine-and-a-half years of my life, which I hardly cherished until they vanished into my past. On that visit in early 1935, Dad told me the story of a dreadful palace massacre that had once occurred there. It has haunted me ever since, driving me to grapple with questions of how such paradoxes of human behavior can exist.

We stood at the top of a watchtower looking down at a teak-walled enclosure, listening to how the mother of Prince Thibaw, one of King Mindon's lesser queens, and Thibaw's wife, Supyalat, gave a reception for all the royal princes, serving them drugged wine. As soon as the princes dropped unconscious, servants loyal to the two evil women, no doubt expecting great rewards for themselves, stuffed the "guests" into dark red velvet sacks (to hide any blood). Without Mindon's knowledge, several of the war elephants were herded in, crushing the "enemy" just as they had been trained to do. Servants shoveled soil onto the bodies and the elephants continued to trample the ground, burying all of Thibaw's rivals. By this elaborate arrangement, the two evil women were able to destroy without "spilling royal blood." Had not the elephants caused the deaths?

The horror of that and other royal massacres I learned of later haunted me, contrasting bitterly with the loving, laughing gentle people I knew and lived among. Dad did not know how King Mindon had reacted, or whether he may have already been too ill to know what had happened. In any case, Thibaw became king.

The easily manipulated Thibaw and his ambitious queen continued to pile up atrocities, giving the British an excuse to intervene. In November 1885, only twenty-eight years after Mindon founded his "Golden City," Thibaw left in exile. The palace was renamed Fort Dufferin, and all Burma became a British colony for the next fifty years. In 1935, most of the royal buildings still housed the British army of Indian soldiers and English officers, while a central core of buildings were kept as a museum. Only ten years later, in March 1945, all this would be reduced to ash, the result of British shelling during World War II to rout the occupying Japanese.

Fifty years later, following my father's death, I found among his books a small English language primer he had bought in Rangoon about 1920. It contained quaint retellings of several legends from *The Glass Palace Chronicles* along with several Jataka tales, and became the immediate catalyst for this collection.

Stories the my Karen "Amah" told me when I was little surfaced, and the realization that my parents could no longer answer questions about those days made me keenly aware of my own mortality. I felt an urgent need to record as many of those memories as possible so my grandchildren might someday share them. Searching for Burma's folk tales became a part of that quest.

At the same time that I was standing awestruck in the palace grounds, Maung Htin Aung, a young graduate student, was traveling through middle Burma, visiting villages near Mandalay and Pagan, listening to folk tales and recording them in his native Burmese. His first volume of about eighty tales, translated into English, was published by Oxford University Press in 1938, just two years after our family returned to America.

His is the most extensive collection of Burmese folk tales I have found anywhere, and approximately half the tales in this book are chosen from that collection. My adaptations modernize his language and add visual details the Burmese storyteller would simply assume his listeners knew. Two other major sources for Burma's stories are *The Glass Palace Chronicles*, already mentioned, and *The Jataka Tales*. These traditional stories came from India along with Buddhism, predating Buddha by many years, perhaps centuries. Because they were much loved, widely known, and morally useful, the Buddhist monks adopted them, renamed them "birth" stories and claimed they told how the Buddha had gradually gained his moral knowledge during his many previous lives. Pictures of these stories, painted on glazed tiles, line the walls of some pagodas where visitors unable to read can at least walk past, recalling the stories and the lessons they taught.

These tales arrived in the Arakan and Mon kingdoms even before the Christian era, and over the centuries some have taken on a peculiarly Burmese character with added bits of Burmese legend or local details. The *Chronicles*, as mentioned before, are a legend-history, taught to young children by the monks along with the Jatakas and the teachings of the Buddha.

In the 1950s Maurice Russell, a schoolmaster from Britain, collected and published a book of Burmese tales told to him by his pupils. Like the schoolbook I found among my father's things, most were Jatakas or legends such as those in the *Chronicles*. Only a few other authors have focused on tales from Burma.

Sadly, my friends tell me, the old tales are being displaced by modern schooling, by entertainment such as movies, and recently by the agitation of troubled times. It thus becomes all the more important for these tales to be preserved in writing and shared even beyond the culture which gave them birth.

For this volume, I have selected thirty-two of the many tales the Burmese love. The tales are retold in the spirit of the original translations and sources. At the beginning of each tale I have added a comment to remind the reader of some historical or cultural fact, or to explain in what way several versions of the story might differ.

In some stories, I have given a Burmese name to The King, The Youth, The Mother, or even The City. But when a particular person or place is named, that name is used in the retelling, with one exception—the story of Ma Chit Su, for whom I chose the name Mistress Beloved.

The Burman storyteller does not bother to add such familiar details as banyans and jacarandas, pagodas and spirit shrines, water jars and stilt-legged bamboo houses unless they have a specific role in the tale. But I have tried to paint a little of Burma's lovely land into each story, and reflect her courteous and gentle people, especially her women— industrious, independent, and greatly respected.

And, for my own sake, because I am a dreamer, the cruelty in some of these stories shall not go unpunished, and kindness shall not go unrewarded—if only in a closing note.

Introduction

Burmese History and Culture

The Burmans called it *Shwe Pyidaw*, the Golden Land, a fertile valley cradled in a horseshoe of mountains. Its kite-shaped boundaries were drawn scarcely more than a hundred years ago, by squabbling Western nations jousting for control of the region's wealth. As a result, four very different ethnic groups—Shans, Chins, Kachins, and Karens, along with their many sub-groups, whose traditional homelands had been in that mountainous arc—found themselves straddling the boundaries of Burma (Myanmar), with many of their closest kin assigned to neighboring Thailand, Laos, China, and India. Only the Burmans, who occupied the great river valleys, lived totally within those artificial boundaries when Britain completed its takeover in 1885.

The Burmans, a Tibeto-Burman people, migrated down the great river valleys of the Chindwin and Irrawaddy during the eighth and ninth centuries, largely to escape new waves of Chinese and Mongolian raids. They absorbed and soon dominated what remained of an earlier related group called Pyu. It was the Burman kings and their kingdom with whom the British bargained and fought. It was their language and their form of Buddhism (Theravada) that has dominated the land for nearly ten centuries. And it is mostly Burman traditional stories that are retold in this volume. The stories are paradoxical—because the people are paradoxical—often infuriatingly so. How do people whose religion is predominantly Buddhist become so obsessed with spirits such as *nats, nagas,* ghosts, and *bilus* (ogres)? Or with astrology, numerology, runes, and oracles—to tell them where to build a house, when to plant and whom to wed?

How do people whose lives and customs at the village level are remarkably egalitarian, who are so given to laughter and gentle courtesies, come to have such Machiavellian kings and generals? How do people who take the Buddha's precept against destroying life so seriously that many will not boil an egg, or breed and harvest silkworms; who despise fishermen, hunters, and butchers for their unholy ways, nevertheless relish meat and fish curries, weave and wear silk as frequently as possible, and listen eagerly to the village storyteller recount the exploits of clever young fishermen, brave hunters, heroes, and villains?

Burma's history is filled with aggressive wars, cruel, often heinous punishments, and superstitious customs that include creating "ghost guardians" by burying people alive under the corners and gateposts of palaces. How can we understand this strange amalgam of ideas and customs? Perhaps the best place to begin is with the Burman Buddhist concept of the cosmos, largely borrowed from India, along with notions of divine kings and, of course, Buddhism itself. The following is a brief retelling from three different, but overlapping, accounts.

In the Beginning

Many universes had come and gone, for these too are bound to the great wheel of existence, and once again all was chaos. At last, rain began falling, first as gentle mist, the drops gradually growing in size until they fell as small stones, then boulders, then splats the size of houses, and finally lake size drops larger than islands, until the rain created the great Thamôddaya Ocean reaching even the abode of the Brahmâs in the sixteen heavens. Bramâh, Brahmâ, Mramma, Myanma, or Mien—various names by which the Burmans have been known over the centuries—all mean "first people."

Soon lotus plants appeared, their starlike flowers rocking on the water. One plant bore five extraordinary blossoms, each of which opened to reveal an orange monk's robe cradled in its center. The gold-tinged edges of the robes glittered, sending rays sparkling through the heavens. Attracted by the dancing light, nine Brahmâs left their heavenly realm to inspect this wonder, and finding the robes, prophesied that in this epoch five Buddhas would emerge. Then they gathered up the holy robes and returned to their abode.

After a time, the lotus plants withered. The water itself rose up, forming buds and flowers and cloudlike patterns, followed by a great scum that gradually hardened into solid land. The land bulged and a great mountain, the Myinmo Taung or Mt. Meru, slowly rose from the waves. Seven ranges of hills encircled it and at the four cardinal points, four large islands formed, each surrounded by five hundred smaller islands.

The sun, moon, and stars, luminous and beautiful, floated high above the islands, circling the great mountain from east to west. But Myinmo rose much higher still, hiding these celestial bodies from each island for half of every day. The northern island was square and glittered with gold, reflecting the golden side of Myinmo. Its inhabitants were blessed spirits who had square, golden faces and lived a thousand youthful years. A sacred tree grew whose boughs hung heavy with succulent food and radiant clothing, providing the spirits with all their needs.

The western island was white and shaped like the full moon, reflecting the silver side of Myinmo. Its inhabitants were also blessed spirits. They had round, white faces and lived lives of ease and pleasure, but for only five hundred years.

Much the same was true of the eastern island. It was shaped like the quarter moon and was green in color, reflecting the glass side of the sacred mountain. Again, the faces of its blessed spirits match the island's shape and color, and a sacred tree supplied every want or need. But the blessed spirits of these three islands were in one way less fortunate than the inhabitants of the fourth island.

This southern island, Jambudipa, (or Zampudipa, after the holy Zampa tree) was at once the most blessed and the most cursed of the four islands. This was our island, the one we humans inhabit. Our light brown trapezoid-shaped faces matched its shape and color and reflected the garnet side of Myinmo Taung. Five great rivers and many small ones flowed down from Jambudipa's mountains, and it was studded with lakes and springs. Garnets and rubies, gold and silver from Myinmo itself lay embedded in the rocks.

Jambudipa was the most cursed of the four islands because it was a world of sorrow whose inhabitants—man, beast, demon or spirit—were all doomed to struggle against the chains of desire, lust, anger, and ignorance, the four great sins. Yet Jambudiya was also the most blessed island, because this struggle provided the only possible path to Ne'ban, the highest level of existence. Only there do the great Buddhas go, bringing knowledge of the unchanging law and teaching the difficult path each soul must travel to reach release from the endless vortex of rebirth.

For eons these islands had no inhabitants, no plants or creatures of any kind, but once the land had been restored, all those realms of existence that had been destroyed in the previous cataclysm now reappeared, bringing the number of realms once again to its full and proper thirty-one.

With all the blissful realms of the Brahmâs restored, their inhabitants now increased greatly. Plants, trees, flowers, shrubs, and grains of all types clothed the land, making it sweet and beautiful. Animals, birds, and aquatic creatures of all types emerged.

The mountain itself exuded a fragrance that wafted high into the heavens. This incense so pleased the Brahmâs that many descended from their realms of bliss, and though their perfect bodies required no food, they tasted the earth, the Myay Thin Ge, and found it sweet. They found golden bowls and cups, hair ornaments and jewelry scattered on the ground or hanging from trees and bushes. The Brahmâs began to gather and use these, and finding them pleasant, wished for more.

With this wish, the first sin, that of desire, was reborn, and the Brahmâs, having lost their innocence, became the first men and women. Not only did they enjoy food, but now their bodies required it. Desire led to craving, and craving led to gluttony. After a time, Earth lost its sweet taste. Instead, a creeping plant called *nwe gyo* grew in abundance. Its licorice taste was so delicious that people gorged on it and soon required a more filling food.

A special paddy called *thalé* replaced the creeper. This rice required no labor, no planting, no reaping. One had only to reach out, and the grains would fall into a person's hand, sweet, tender, and ready to eat. But the eating of rice soon changed people physically. Male and female genitals developed and the people began to feel lust.

Some, giving thought to the changes that had followed their desire for sweet food and glittering ornaments, reasoned that this new pleasure might in turn bring further evils. These few deliberately refrained from yielding to their new passions and tried to warn others. Quarrels broke out between those with differing opinions, until at last the people counseled together, and marriage was instituted in an attempt to find harmony between lust and abstention.

But lust had already brought more sorrow into the world.

At first, no matter how much *thalé* the people cut to eat each day, the fields regrew at night and were full once again the next morning. But soon the *thalé* no longer replenished itself. Now people had to plant, harvest, thrash, and cook the grains. To sustain life, the people had to labor and sweat and endure pain and fatigue.

Anger, insult, theft, adultery, even murder—crimes of every type—plagued the land, and all the hells burst gleefully into flame, anticipating the first victims. But still the people did not understand that these great sorrows had arrived through their own ignorance, which was the greatest sin of all.

In their distress, the people sought someone to guide them, mediate their quarrels, and punish those who disturbed the harmony. They found one among them who was especially wise, pious, just, and compassionate—and asked him to lead them.

Thus the first king was appointed. He came to be called Mahathamada, and was a *Payalaung*; that is, he was destined to become the epoch's first Buddha.

Today the universe is in its declining phase, the only one in which the Buddhas appear. They come to mitigate the earth's constantly increasing burden of evil. Four have come already, the last being Shin Gautama. In another 2,500 years, the fifth and last Buddha will come and after the time of his influence, everything will once again be destroyed.

Fire will consume the universe if greed, gluttony, and avarice predominate. Water will wash it away if lust and anger rule. But if ignorance, the greatest evil of all, prevails, the universe will be swept away by a great wind.

Fire, water, and wind: all three can destroy, but only water can create. Then chaos will rule until the gentle rains begin to fall once again.

Buddha and the Cosmos

2,500 years ago, Siddhartha Gautama, fourth Buddha of the current epoch, directed his entire meditation toward understanding the universal condition of suffering and defining "right behavior" and "right thought." He was not interested in spirits and demigods or with theories about the shape, size, or evolution of the cosmos.

He dismissed the pantheon of Hindu gods and the epic tales of Rama and other heroes as irrelevant superstition, teaching that each soul makes its own karma. Asking for favors from nonexistent gods, he preached, was wasted effort. Instead, one should spend time meditating on the "perfect" and learning to avoid desire in any form. Only this, he believed, could free man from the vortex of endless rebirth into the world of sorrow—a Hindu concept he clearly accepted as "given."

Three times each day, a devout Buddhist sought strength to follow "the right path" by repeating "The Three Jewels":

I take refuge in the Buddha (the enlightened one).

I take refuge in the Dharma (the precepts he taught).

I take refuge in the Sangha (the brotherhood of monks).

In addition, every good Buddhist hoped someday to build a pagoda, or at least honor a shrine with flowers or a new patch of gold leaf. If a person behaved in a righteous way, he would gain merit, but if he behaved in an evil way, he would acquire "demerit." At death the balance between these would determine his next existence: maybe a higher or lower position in society, rebirth as a lowly worm or a noble elephant, entry into the realms of the blessed beings or even *Ne'ban.*

The Thirty-One Levels of Existence

Arupa-Loka: The Four Planes of "Non-Matter":
These beings are pure thought, with no form or physical existence:
Level 31: "Ne'ban," the realm of "neither perception nor non-perception"
Level 30: "Nothingness"
Level 29: "The infinity of Consciousness"
Level 28: "The infinity of Space"

Rupa-Loka: The Sixteen Planes of "Subtle Matter"
Here the inhabitants are luminous and perfect. Having left all physical need behind, they feed on joy, love by the presence of the beloved, and are born without the intervention of parents or sex. *Levels 12 to 27:* This is the abode of the Brahmâs. When worlds are destroyed, fire, water, or winds sweep away all the lower levels reaching into the lower planes of Rupa-Loka.

Kama-Loka: The Eleven Planes of "Sensual Beings"
Levels 6-11: The Six Heavens of the Blessed Spirits. The planes of pleasure. Nats, Dewas, Galons, Garudas, and spirits of many kinds dwell here, inhabiting Mount Myinmo, the sun, moon, and stars, earthly places on Jampudipa such as mountain tops, trees, streams, lakes, etc.
Level 7: Myinmo Taung rises high into the seventh plane. Many spirits choose to live here.
Level 6: Sun, moon, and stars exist in the sixth level, constantly circling the great mountain, and shining in turn on each of the four great islands. But one half of each day they are blocked from view as they travel around the far side of Myinmo. They are the chosen home of many blessed spirits.
Levels 1-5: The Five Planes of Suffering
Level 5: The Human Plane
Level 4: The Animal Plane
Level 3: The Plane of Bilus (ogres), ghosts, witches, and despicable beings.
Levels 1 and 2: The eight great hells and the 40,040 lesser ones. When they first came into being, the walls and floors were smooth, hard iron. Later the surface levels corroded into soft soil, and after evil re-entered the world, the hells burst into flames.

This belief in rebirth is illustrated in the "legend-history" of Burma's early kings. Three of these kings were exceptionally erratic, vain, given to fits of temper and wholly unsuited to rule. Rebirth offered the explanation.

According to the legend, an ogre once saw a man resting nearby, hot and exhausted. Moved by the man's aura of goodness, the ogre plucked three large leaves to shade him. The Buddha, for it was he, thanked the ogre for his kindness and prophesied that in the future the ogre would thrice become king of Burma. What could one expect of a king who had once been an ogre?

To what further extent ancient Hindu beliefs influenced Shin Gautama's teachings, only a scholar of that religion would be able to say, but certainly the ancient tales and beliefs were deep in the psyche of many of his followers, and other aspects of Hindu belief, including cosmology, came to Burma along with the Buddhist monks.

As to the cosmos, there was a geography taught by the monks and accepted by most Burmans until at least the end of the nineteenth century. In it, Jambudipa, the southern island, corresponded roughly to Eurasia. Burma was its largest, most important portion, and Burmans were the direct descendants of those first Brahmâs who came down from the heavens.

For proof that all this was true, one only had to observe how the sun, moon, and stars appeared daily from the east and disappeared to the west behind Myinmo's great height. This concept of geography led the kings of Burma to view foreigners as savages, unimportant and unworthy of serious consideration. Ironically, since ignorance was considered the greatest evil, this concept contributed to the disastrous decisions of Narathihapate Min in 1257, ending the First Burmese Empire, and Thibaw Min in 1885, ending the Third Burmese Empire and beginning Burma's period of colonial rule.

Empires: Three Moments in Time

In and near the northern tip of Burma, the great Himalayan arc curves abruptly into an accordion of north-south ranges whose deep gorges hold some branch, tributary, or source of five great rivers. These embryonic rivers then fan outward into most of the lands known to the ancient Burman world.

One, the Brahmaputra, flows west into India, joining the Ganges. One is, or joins, the Yangtze River, flowing east into China. One is a source of the Mekong, flowing southeast into Laos, Thailand, Cambodia, and Vietnam. And two, the Salween and Irrawaddy, along with the latter's major tributary, the Chindwin, flow into the broad fertile plains and rich delta lands of Burma. Several of these rivers have mirror twins flowing north from the divide into central Mongolia. Together, the north- and south-flowing rivers create a corridor through the forbidding mountain ranges.

There is also a difficult east-west passage through northern Burma, which was once part of the ancient "silk road." In World War II, Allied Forces made use of that route, building the Ledo leading northwest from Myitkyina (Myi-chen-ah) across the Naga hills into India, and the Burma Road leading northeast from Nam Kam into China's Yunnan Province.

However, it was the migrations down the Irrawaddy, each group vying for control of the river and its broad fertile plain, that formed the matrix of Burma's history. And within that history, three-course changing events molded Burman thought and action.

1. Chinese slave raids into Central Asia and Tibet (B.C. and the first millennium) with the subsequent migration of Burman tribes, who paused for refuge in Nan Chao (Yunnan).

2. The conversion of Anawrahta Min to Theravada Buddhism, initiating the "Golden Age" of Pagan (Pay-gahn).

3. British occupation of Burma, leading to the current bitter crisis of redefinition.

Period One: Migrations

During the last three millennia, three major groups: Mon-Khmer, Pyu-Burman, and Shan-Thai, as well as many minor ones, migrated down the river valleys from their harsh steppe or mountain homes into Burma's fertile plain.

The Mon arrived first, sometime in the first millennium B.C., followed a few centuries later by their Khmer kin. From Central Asia they traveled along the Salween and Mekong rivers, largely displacing the aboriginal tribes whose possible descendents are still found in small enclaves in remote hill areas and islands to the south.

The Mon (or Talaing) were wet rice farmers who settled mostly along the coasts, rivers and deltas of Burma, Laos, Cambodia, and Thailand. By 500 B.C., they had built a flourishing civilization with literature, music, architecture, and art, much of which was influenced by their extensive sea trading contacts with India, whose culture was at a peak. Mon craftsmen included skilled gold- and silversmiths, as well as wood, ivory, and jade carvers. They built pagodas and temples with brick, but did not yet use the arch. Whatever beliefs they brought from the Asian steppes, the Mon were thoroughly Buddhist by 300 B.C., practicing the demanding Theravada precepts.

About the first century A.D., a Tibeto-Burman people called Pyu began to arrive. Moving east and south from Mongolia and Tibet, they pushed the Mon farther south and for a time out of central Burma. Legend claims the Pyu founded the city of Pagan in A.D. 108 and archeologists date Sri Ksetra (near modern Prome) even earlier.

Jousting between Mon and Pyu control continued until, in the eighth century, the Pyu were pushed northward, briefly establishing a capital at Halin. At this same time, the Shan-Thai of Nan Chao (Yunnan) began to expand. Groups of Thai migrated down the Mekong and its adjacent lands, while the Shan poured down the Salween, spreading across the Shan plateau and even into the Irrawaddy plain. In A.D. 832, they conquered the Pyu capital of Halin, enslaving most of the population and dispersing the rest.

Meanwhile, Burman tribes also began moving rapidly down the Irrawaddy and Chindwin, soon establishing themselves at Pagan, where they could control the river and thus the great rice plain. Like their Pyu kin, they had originated in the highlands near the China-Tibet border and spoke a similar but not identical language. In their highland home they had become prime prey for Chinese slave raiders. To protect their families, they began to leave, hoping to find a safer homeland.

For a while, the Burmans had taken refuge in Nan Chao where they learned wet-rice-farming techniques, animal husbandry, and new fighting skills, but retained their long established attitudes and culture. Traditionally, Burmans governed themselves by alliances of villages called "circles" based on matrilineal kinship. They held their women in high regard and social prestige was won through behavior rather than ownership.

As Buddhism spread north and east from India, the deeply ingrained animism of the indigenous people combined readily with Buddhism's Tantric forms, which included considerable remnants of Hindu beliefs in spirits, gods, and demigods. Hinduism itself had evolved over the centuries by assimilating various spirit cults, such as Naga or snake cults connected with Shiva the destroyer. However, these cults were "place dependent," giving great power to local priests, astrologers, and magicians.

Buddha had taught that "salvation" from the wheel of suffering was achieved by one's own action, not by the intervention of some priest. This concept of freedom and personal responsibility was a very attractive idea and a major factor in the spread of Buddhism. But within a few hundred years, power was quickly reclaimed by priests and spiritual mediums who reintroduced magical rites and many popular gods. With a gift to the right intermediary, one did not have to work so hard following the "path of righteous living." One could buy one's way into the higher levels of blessedness. In the Tibetan highlands, the Burman people had acquired a thin layer of this Tantric Buddhism, called Mahayana, bringing it with them into the Golden Land.

However, one faction called Theravada, or "The Way of the Elders," remained close to Buddha's teachings as recorded by his disciples. Wide popular knowledge of these scriptures known as the *Tripitaka*, or "three baskets," was encouraged. Holy men were not considered priests, instead, they were respected as contemplative monks and teachers. They schooled the young, tried to discipline themselves to Buddhist ideals and shared their insight with those who sought advice. The center for this Theravada doctrine was Ceylon (Sri Lanka), and the Mon kingdom of Thaton was its strong satellite.

Period II: Anawrahta Min (1044 to 1077)

The "Glory of Pagan" began with Anawrahta. At the start of his reign, this small Burman city was the capital of a culturally simple kingdom, while to the south, in the Irrawaddy delta, the Mon kingdom of Thaton flourished. No doubt Anawrahta was well aware of its riches and culture even before the Mon king of Pegu, Thaton's rival, asked him and his Burman troops to help ward off a Cambodian invasion, an alliance Thaton's king opposed.

Anawrahta was an extraordinary general. He was the first to train and use war elephants, and his well-disciplined forces not only repulsed the Cambodian forces, but in 1057 also overwhelmed Thaton. This conquest united upper and lower Burma for the first time, creating the First Burmese Empire.

As booty, Anawrahta took king, court, and skilled craftsmen of every sort—30,000 prisoners in all—to Pagan. He had the holy writings—the *Tripitaka*—loaded onto elephants and brought along with the entire *Sangha* (Brotherhood of Monks) to his capital. There he built new monasteries for the monks, dedicating most of his other prisoners to them and the Buddha as pagoda slaves. He placed the defeated king, his queen, and some courtiers in a small guarded palace where they lived effectively under "house arrest."

Whether Anawrahta had heard the Mon monk, Shin Arahan, teach before this conquest is uncertain, but clearly the holy man's preaching deeply affected him, and soon the Shin became his closest advisor. Together they set out to convert the entire kingdom, and conqueror became the conquered as Mon culture soon permeated every aspect of life in Anawrahta's newly flourishing capital.

First of all, probably as a political move, Anawrahta had himself installed king in the Hindu mystical manner, making himself a demigod, an avatar of Vishnu, the first Burman leader to do this. Quite possibly, the chronicles that make him a descendent of the Pyu kings were also "adjusted" at this time. Certainly at some point the legend-histories of the Pyu kings merged with Burman tradition.

Anawrahta wanted the holy scriptures available to all his people. With the help of Shin Arahan and the monks, an alphabet was devised based on, but not the same as, Pali script. Using this new alphabet, they translated the Pali scriptures into Burmese. Now young boys who went daily to the monasteries to recite the holy words learned to read as well.

But for all his holy passions, Anawrahta was short-tempered. In the legends, his quick anger appears again and again. According to those legends, Anawrahta was the son of a deposed king. As a young man he took service with the reigning king, his cousin, who one day insulted him publicly. This humiliation sent Anawrahta to his father, now a holy hermit, to ask for the magic ruby, sword, spear, and horse that Thagya Min, the Spirit King, had once given his father. Anawrahta then went to holy Mount Popa to raise an army, which he led against Pagan. In the ensuing battle he killed his cousin, becoming the next king.

This death, and the many caused by his battles, troubled him. Killing was against the precepts of Buddha. The deaths would bring him many demerits, dooming him to unspeakable status in his next life. Shin Arahan comforted him, explaining that wrongdoing could be balanced by pious acts. Why not build pagodas to the glory of Buddha and the Great Truth?

Thus a flurry of temple building began on the plains of Pagan.

Kyanzittha continued his father's work, bringing Pagan's Golden Age to a peek, further unifying the empire with both conquest and astute political moves.

Legends resembling Tristram and Isolde are told about both father and son. Anawrahta's first queen was the princess Pyinsa Kalyani of Wethali in Northern India. Anawrahta sent a young envoy to escort his future bride to Pagan. En route, the envoy fell in love with her. Scheming to win the beautiful princess for himself, he dismissed her attendants a few at a time during the journey.

Meanwhile, the king traveled to meet his betrothed queen in Arakan, where their marriage was consummated. But the envoy hinted that the lovely young woman could not possibly be a real princess or her father would have sent a large, regal retinue to escort her. King Anawrahta burst into a fit of temper at the thought of such insult to him, a great king. He promptly exiled his bride to a distant town where his soldiers were to keep her under heavy guard, dashing the envoy's amorous hopes.

Soon it was clear the queen was pregnant, but neither king nor envoy knew of this. Anawrahta refused to hear any word about this woman who had brought him such dishonor, and the envoy was equally barred from news. When Kyanzittha, the queen's child was born, a great quake shook the earth. As earthquakes were always a portent of some tragedy or great event, King Anawrahta called his astrologers and soothsayers, who consulted their books and charts. A child had just been born, they said, who would one day rule Pagan.

Anawrahta flew into a great rage. No usurper would live to dethrone him if he could help it. He asked where this had happened. Again the astrologers huddled over their charts. Near Payeinma, they told him.

Unaware that this was the very place his exiled his queen was imprisoned, the king sent soldiers to kill every infant in or near there. Miraculously, mother and child escaped, helped by a Naga youth. The legend goes on to tell how the king later discovered that Kyanzittha, the wonder-child, was his own son. Deeply ashamed, he took mother and son back into the palace.

Kyanzittha grew up to become one of four young heroes, each mounted, like the king, on spirit-horses given by Thagya Min, the spirit king. Anawrahta Min and his young heroes became known far and wide for their brave invincibility, riding at the head of armies, conquering city after city.

A few years later, Anawrahta was to wed again. This time he sent Kyanzittha to escort the prospective bride, but when they returned, Anawrahta, noticing the glances exchanged between his son and his betrothed, again flew into a rage. Believing Kyanzittha had seduced the princess, Anawrahta had him bound, intending to kill him himself. But when he threw his magic spear, the power of the Spirit King diverted it, causing it to cut Kyanzittha's bonds without wounding him in any way. Kyanzittha escaped and fled.

Following Anawrahta's death, Kyanzittha's half-brother, Sawlu, became king. Kyanzittha returned, offering to serve Sawlu as he had their father. As before, he showed extraordinary military skills. But, jealous and insecure, Sawlu was constantly suspicious, distrusting Kyanzittha's advice. As a result, Sawlu was defeated in a battle with the Mons and taken prisoner.

Loyally attempting to rescue his king, Kyanzittha stole

into the Mon stronghold one night. But ever suspicious, Sawlu thought Kyanzittha had come to kill him and shouted for help. The disgusted Kyanzittha fled to safety, but the guards promptly killed Sawlu themselves to prevent any further rescue attempts.

That much is legend. History shows that Kyanzittha, the next king, became an intelligent leader and a great builder, both of national unity and splendid pagodas. He continued his father's efforts to oust the Tantric Ari monks and replace their doctrine with Theravada beliefs. Shin Arahan, the same monk who had been Anawrahta's closest advisor, now advised the son.

Because animism and *nat*-spirit worship were prevalent and deeply ingrained, the decision was made to select and endorse a group of thirty-six particularly popular *nats*, adding a thirty-seventh, a King of Nats patterned on legends about Sakka (Sakra, Sakya, or Indra). Together, monks and kings embellished the life stories of each *nat*, making him or her into a devout follower of the Buddha. The tactic only slightly tamed the hold of animism. Astrology, numerology, and reliance on soothsayers continued to dominate both court and commoner, and does to this day.

Within the next two centuries, building and religious activity changed Pagan into a splendid city, known far and wide as "The City of 400 Million Pagodas" (actually about 13,000 including monasteries and other religious buildings).

By this time, Kublai Khan was vastly extending his empire southward. Conquest brought prestige and great wealth in the form of tribute from vassal kingdoms. The Khan, like Anawrahta and Kyanzittha, was a very religious man. He knew of Pagan, its magnificent pagodas and intriguing religion. He sent the young Venetian merchant, Marco Polo, to Pagan and other Southeast Asian capitals with orders to bring him descriptions of how these other people lived and believed. Pleased with Marco's reports, the Khan sent an offer of peace to these kingdoms on condition they agree to send him annual tribute.

At that time, Narathihapate, whose former name was Kwéchi Min (Prince Dirty Dog) was Pagan's king. He was one of the three Mins who legend says were reincarnations of a *bilu*. In fact, the man was paranoid and quite mad, and when the Khan's envoys arrived, he not only assumed the Mongol forces were insignificant but insulted them as well. Accordingly, the Khan's army advanced, destroying the main Burmese forces in a battle well north of the royal city. Narathihapate panicked, and fearing the Mongols would rape his court women, he ordered them tied and thrown into the river to drown. He then fled the city before the Mongol army entered.

The "destruction" of Pagan appears to be in large part the result of the Burmans themselves tearing down pagodas to build fortifications, though the Mongols certainly did loot the empty city.

The Mongol empire shrank almost as quickly as it had expanded, and the void was filled by resurgent Shan and Mon kingdoms. The First Burmese Empire no longer existed, but two hundred years had vastly changed Burman culture, perhaps even more than the sojourn in Yunnan some seven or eight hundred years earlier.

Not for another six hundred years would there be an equally significant change in Burma's view of the world.

Period III: Western Impact

From the fifteenth century on, European traders began to arrive in considerable numbers throughout Southeast Asia, but this early contact had only minor effects on these cultures. Then, during the nineteenth century, the British gained control in increments, beginning with Tenasserim and Arakan in 1824, Lower Burma and Rangoon (Yangon) in 1846, and finally Mandalay and Upper Burma in 1885—giving Britain control of all Burma.

Most of the incoming British were every bit as myopic as the Burmans. They saw a people who laughed easily, enjoyed festivals, napped during the middle of the day, worked at a leisurely pace, and they declared them "lazy." In the public squares and open spaces they saw men who did little between planting and harvest other than lounge, smoke, and play dominoes, but overlooked the many others busy in their home gardens, or scouring the hillsides for firewood, or crafting beautiful items in some workshop.

They gave small heed to the debilitating chronic malaria, tropical diseases, and nutritional deficiencies (particularly calcium and niacin) that left the Burmese already old at forty. And they completely overlooked Burma's enterprising, industrious women. What the British did see was a land rich with rice, teak, tin, and rubies, and a people doing nothing (from the British point of view) with all this wealth. They saw simple housing and pre-industrial crafts and interpreted it as poverty, where in fact, food and the materials for simple living were available to all. Virtually no one was hungry, homeless, or in rags and tatters. They saw a people gazing devoutly at alabaster idols and declared them pagan and in need of the "true" religion. They simply administered Burma as a province of British India, ignoring local customs and beliefs as interesting but unimportant. Theirs was the "White Man's Burden," to raise these "savages" to English, or at least Western, sensibilities.

The incoming British arrived with their Indian servants, soldiers, and clerks. They set up huge mechanical mills, paid the farmers well for their rice harvest, and began the unintentional impoverishment of Burma's farmers that continues to the present day.

As British exporters bid to buy rice, the farmers began to borrow to buy more land and seed, hoping to have more to sell. But of course not every year's harvest was a good one. Money-lenders, mostly Indians who had arrived with the British, often charged up to one hundred percent interest.

One by one, farmers defaulted on their loans, forfeiting the mortgaged land while the British caretaker government did nothing effective to intervene. This was simply "free enterprise" running its natural course, and in the 1800s most Europeans believed passionately in the "invisible hand." Everyone would benefit in the long run—or so they thought.

Instead, vast numbers of Burmans soon became tenant-farmers on what had once been their own land. This spurred riots against Burma's Indian population and fed movements to win independence from Britain.

As colonial masters, the British did have several practices in their favor. Taking a leaf from the Romans before them, they trained indigenous people to fill many clerical and minor administrative positions. They recruited and drilled local people as soldiery. And they established the British system of law based on a respect for every individual—even if the deed did not always match the intention.

For all this, an educated class was required. The Burmans had a long tradition of schooling every boy (and sometimes girls) at least enough to recognize the Burmese alphabet and a few passages of Buddhist scripture, so the new British state schools and American mission schools were mostly well received. But of course, with Western schooling, Western medicine, Western religious views, and Western law came new, conflicting ideas of geography and science and the world in general.

Only a few Burmese youth came from families wealthy enough to allow them to attend high school and then go on to universities in Rangoon, Oxford, or Cambridge. But these were already the young men and women most likely to be the country's future leaders. Meanwhile, most children continued to attend the local monastery school, reciting scriptures, chanting the alphabet, and continuing to hear how Mount Myinmo blocked the sun, moon, and stars for half of each day.

Yet, by 1930 Burma had changed irrevocably, and even more drastic change was soon to come.

Crisis

Many British, certain of their superiority, expected to be addressed as Thakin, meaning lord. The British excluded Burmans from the army and other choice positions, giving these places instead to Karens, a rival ethnic minority. School and civil service exams were given only in English, handicapping many bright young men. Groups calling for varying measures of reform and independence began to form.

That year a group of thirty young students at Rangoon University formed a political alliance, calling themselves "The Thirty Thakins" to emphasize their equality with the British and stress their intrinsic human worth. They studied Marxism, knew of and respected the American struggle for independence, and admired the American constitution. They had grown beyond a simple return to the old days of kings. Many Western ideas seemed worthy, but a new Burma would need a marriage between the best of both worlds. The Thakins were united in striving to regain an independent Burma, but their visions for its future later proved disparate.

The young Thakin Aung San was one of several who sought alliance with Japan. In turn Japan courted the Thakins, agreeing to help them free Burma from the British. These young Thakins were naive, but not stupid. They soon realized that the Japanese generals said one thing, but did another. Experience quickly showed that the Japanese military would just be a new, and very much more cruel, master whose attitudes and beliefs were far from democratic.

Aung San secretly contacted the British, and the Thakins and their forces rejoined Allied efforts to sweep out the Japanese. But following the end of World War II, Burma disintegrated into battling factions. Some of these were ethnic minorities seeking separate destinies, others followed ideological banners: communist, anti-communist, socialist, democratic. And compounding matters, the Kuomintang Chinese Nationalists of Chiang Kai-shek took refuge in northern Burma during China's bitter revolution.

In 1947 the Burmans and most of the minorities reached a compromise. They wrote a constitution creating a democratic government, and a few months later the British parliament voted to grant their independence. But like Moses, Aung San was to be denied the "Promised Land." On July 19, 1947, members of a jealous faction shot and killed Aung San along with several others.

Six months later, on January 4, 1948, Burma finally gained its long-sought independence. U Nu became president, and for a time the world looked on hopefully as the young government attempted land and other reforms. Burma continued, though, to be torn by its quarreling factions.

In 1958, Ne Win, also one of the original Thakins, was asked to take temporary command. At first his efforts brought a measure of stability, but soon he realized his single-minded vision for Burma's future was not shared by all. By 1962 Ne Win decided that the disorder of democracy with all its messy debates and protests would destroy his beloved land. He simply declared himself supreme leader and imposed "law and order" by force, ousting all Europeans, most Indians and many of the better-educated Burmans.

He then moved determinedly forward, doing what was good for Burma, as he saw it. He carried "land reform" still further, often forcibly moving whole villages to make room for "progress." But as few of his generals had the knowledge to run their departments well, bureaucratic inefficiency rose to new heights.

This devoted "socialist," who had preached vigorously against exploitation and inequality, had become a cruel dictator, impoverishing his nation by selling Burma's resources to support his army and greatly enrich himself.

On the plus side, Ne Win's isolation did succeed in keeping Burma out of the alignment wars plaguing the other Southeast Asian countries—Vietnam, Cambodia, and Laos.

The government bureaus genuinely tried to improve schooling, farming and hygiene, however ineptly, and many approved. Besides, as many Burmans say of their army even today, "They are our sons."

It was the minorities, the remaining intellectuals, and other dissenters who felt the heel of the military boot most heavily.

In 1981 Ne Win resigned, but was succeeded by San Yu, still part of the military junta. By 1988 a general strike brought matters to a head. Daw Aung San Suu Kyi, daughter of General Aung San, was among the voices calling loudly for elections. Ne Win himself spoke to the nation, agreeing to hold elections, though it was many more months before they actually occurred.

Meanwhile, Daw Suu Kyi and others in the National League for Democracy traveled the country, drawing large, eager crowds. Five months before the elections took place the junta, fearing people's positive response to this outspoken woman, placed Daw Suu Kyi under house arrest. In addition, the junta declared her ineligible for office because she was married to an Englishman, a foreigner, claiming this put the nation's secrets at risk.

The elections were finally held in May 1990, and Daw Suu Kyi and her party won an overwhelming majority of the seats in parliament: eighty-one percent. But the junta, which had expected an easy win for themselves, annulled the results and tightened its control once more.

This brave, obstinate woman follows in the footsteps of her honored ancestors. Government authorities have told her she is free to leave Burma, but not free to stay, moving about the country, stirring up "unrest." She chooses to stay on, speaking out against the military dictatorship from her home whenever possible.

In 1991, Daw Suu Kyi received the Nobel Peace prize for her outspoken persistence. She shares her father's dream of a democratic Burma in which all people and beliefs are equally respected. Meanwhile, at the end of the twentieth century, Burma remains poised between that hope and its present oppressive regime.

Village and Town: The Common People

In 1882, a Scot who had come to Burma as a teacher wrote what is probably still the definitive description of the Burman people in his book, *The Burman; His Life and Notions*. In it he described the common experiences of mind and place that inform the folk tales in this volume.

For centuries, that portrait remained much the same, but following the arrival of the British, Burma began changing; a change that has accelerated greatly during the past fifty years. As most recent books and articles focus primarily on those changes, it is diffficult for the reader to see a whole picture of the land.

What changes are superficial? What remains basic? And what has shifted unalterably?

In the past, village life went on almost independently of royalty or the British governors. The ancient pattern of matrilineally related villages, five to each cluster or "circle," continued, and people quietly went about their own affairs.

A *Thugyi* (village head man) held the role of elder or advisor, and the *Myothugyi* (head man for the circle of five villages) convened the people when group decisions were required. All the adults participated in a discussion of what action to take. This element of democracy in a people who often endured despotic kings may yet provide the quiet strength Burma needs to weather its current crisis.

Village Landscape

Today, as they did long ago, dike-bordered rice fields stretch all along the wide flood plain of the Irrawaddy and other major rivers of central Burma, making a great green-and-blue quilt of grasses when Burma is wet, gradually turning amber and bronze as the land dries and the grain ripens. Here and there, palm trees dot the plain and villages hide in thickets of trees—an oasis of shade created by the farmers themselves.

In these thickets, a handful of bamboo houses crouch on stilt legs, clustered along both sides of a dirt road that is scarcely more than a rutted bullock cart trail. Under the houses, jungle hens scratch and roosters strut. Semi-feral dogs, called "pi-dogs" by the English and "kwé" by the Burmese, sniff through garbage piles and around the house posts. The dogs gaze mournfully at the village children, hoping for a pat or a tidbit. A Burmese cat, gaunt and angular, slinks through the bushes stalking a ground squirrel.

Crows and sparrows bathe in the dust. A peacock fans his tail, squawking his lordly status. A goat meanders from house to house, browsing on *tapari* bushes or carelessly forgotten slippers.

Out in the paddy fields, a great gray water buffalo stoically heaves the farmer's plow forward through the mud. Cattle egrets step unconcernedly near its large hoofs, feasting on ticks from the animal's ear, or gulping grasshoppers and gnats that scatter in its wake. Nearby, several boys splash and play in a wallow, taking turns on the neck of a buffalo calf.

An oxcart, drawn by a team of scrawny white Brahma bullocks, creaks along the rutted ochre road, its approach announced by piercing screeches from spokeless wheels and the clunk of wooden ox-bells. The carter, an Indian dressed in dingy white bombees, idly prods his team forward. Neither man nor ox seem much concerned with speed. The sun is already high, and the day is oppressively hot.

This is the dry zone, the region from which most of the stories in this volume have come.

Between the village and the hazy blue hills to the east, magpies sit on stunted thorn trees, or acacias, scolding passing snakes, lizards, or field mice. Vultures circle over the desiccated carcass of a mongoose or a jackal. And in a wooded patch nearby, monkeys chatter excitedly.

Many village families tend a house garden, raising vegetables, flowers, and fruits to eat and sell. There may be jasmine—white, pink, or red– twin-petaled golden "butterfly bush," purple asters, cosmos, carnations, and scarlet canna lilies, or fruits such as banana, mango, papaya, and pomolo (ancestor to the grapefruit).

The street may be shaded by padauk trees, whose clusters of golden blossoms predict the rains, jacaranda blooming lavender in cool February, fragrant white frangipani, tamarind, banyan or above all, "Pride of India" or flame tree, blazing scarlet during the hottest months.

Tall palms, thickets of bamboo, and perhaps a few forest trees such as breadfruit, jackfruit, pink-flowered koko trees or even teak, grow in one village or another. All these are chosen for their particular beauty or perfume, turning the whole village into a refuge from Burma's punishing sun.

Beyond the village, an assortment of weeds and grasses grow sparsely under the blistering heat but spring to new life with the coming of the rains. Water lilies, hyacinth, watercress, and rushes choke the ponds. And where a hill lifts above the blanket of heat, lantana, tapari, raspberry, and wild roses all thrive. To announce the cool months, great banks of poinsettia bloom on the slopes. Here, also, tall stands of eucalyptus join clumps of bamboo.

Higher still are the forests where wild elephants splash in streams and captive ones harvest teak, each animal directed by its *oozie* (*mahaut* or driver) who is groom, trainer, and lifelong friend to the great beast.

In the delta, part of Burma's wet zone, villages are much the same except that jungle and swamp prevail. Here brilliantly colored birds screech, crocodiles glide through bayous, and again, the ubiquitous monkeys mock, mimic, and race among the branches. Dusty or soggy, the "Golden Land" is quite beautiful.

The House and its Furnishings

The land offers both the Burman and his hill-dwelling neighbors abundant materials for a simple, satisfying life, starting with that unique grass, bamboo.

Pushing a barrow or riding a hired bullock cart, a man wishing to build a house will travel a dozen or so miles to find his material. With sure, strong strokes of his *dah*—a knife which is both tool and weapon—he will cut large sturdy stalks for the frame and flooring, dozens more of green supple ones for the mat walls, and a quantity of strong liana vine for binding. Construction will take a week or two, perhaps less if his wife or a relative helps.

The choice of support poles is based on centuries-old beliefs as well as practical engineering. A pole is "male" or "female," "demon" or "benign," depending on whether it tapers upward, downward, bulges, or is perfectly straight. Additionally, the pole's nature presumably interacts with forces in the earth, which the local astrologer will interpret for a fee.

One of the "demon" poles will be intentionally chosen and positioned near the doorway to protect the family from other passing demons. Four to six poles support the longer front and back walls, while two or three suffice for the ends. These are set firmly into the earth, often with some good luck token buried at their base.

The floor rests several feet above ground level and is made of mid-sized bamboo, split in halves and secured round side up over the lateral supports. No one seems to mind the corrugated result, and such flooring makes housekeeping easy. Food crumbs simply fall through the cracks to the ground below.

To form the walls, the young bamboo stalks will be sliced into thin strips, which are then woven into mats about six feet high and four feet wide. Husband and wife often work side by side, taking pride in their skillful, airy designs. Window or door spaces are woven right into the panel. Like the frame, these panels are tied securely in place with strong vine, using traditional knots that have proven reliable over the centuries. An open space between the top of each wall mat and the beginning of the roof provides extra ventilation.

Finally the roof is thatched. Both hip and ridge roofs are common, with perhaps more of the former. Thatch material varies with the area of the country. In the wet delta area a leafy plant is chosen, while in the dry region a special grass is used. This grass has the unique quality of shrinking when it is dry and hot, allowing air to circulate, but swelling into a waterproof mass during the rains.

Corrugated tin, manufactured near Burma's tin mines, was, at least for a time, quite fashionable in the towns, but it is a poor choice. Tin intensifies the heat. Also, it corrodes and is expensive to replace.

The houses in towns are usually teakwood and constructed by hired carpenters, but the basic pattern remains much the same. In the past, kings forbade the use of brick or stone for houses, but that changed with the incoming British, who brought nostalgic thoughts of home. In Rangoon (Yangon), streets are lined with Victorian brick buildings, from warehouses to universities, many more than a century old. At least the British had the good sense to build the ceilings high. But for that matter, so did Burma's kings—and long before the two cultures had any knowledge of one another.

The traditional bamboo village house is perfectly suited to Burma's sub-tropical climate. Mat walls are airy, and their elevation invites what little breeze might wander past during the stifling hot season. But more importantly, the stilt legs hold the house above mud and flood during the heavy monsoon rains. The raised floor also reduces the likelihood of rats or snakes inviting themselves in. Although these creatures can and do climb up the house poles, at least the floor is not directly in their path.

As for tigers, they are extinct today in most areas. But in the past, when a tiger prowled near a village hoping to capture a goat or water buffalo, the stilt houses kept the village children high and out of reach.

The basic house has one large rectangular room and usually a *downjah*, a low sleeping platform built across one end. Windows at each end allow cross-ventilation. At the front is the door, with a bamboo ladder to reach it, and perhaps an additional window.

Most houses also have a veranda, frequently one in back and one in front. These are built a foot or two lower than the floor of the house, requiring a step up into the large main room. Later the husband might screen off a private bed space as the family starts to grow. Sometimes an extra room is built and used as a kitchen, but more often cooking takes place outdoors or in a separate small building, leaving the main house cooler.

Furnishings are simple, giving the rooms a spacious look, and like the house itself, most items can be made or purchased inexpensively. Of prime importance is the altar for the Buddha statue, perhaps a small shelf or three-legged table of carved teak set near the door.

Shelter for the night is of course the *sine qua non* of any home. Bedding consists of woven mats and cotton blankets spread each evening on the raised *downjah* then rolled away out of sight in the morning. Today most families also suspend cotton netting over themselves to discourage mosquitoes.

The soft glow of a traditional clay oil lamp or a hissing kerosene lantern provides light. And although today cities and many towns have been electrified for a number of years, lighting fixtures remain mostly unsophisticated. Bare incandescent bulbs and harsh fluorescent tubes decorate shops and even outline some pagodas.

Each household has several wooden chests, usually made of teak or other insect-resistant wood, to hold clothing and personal possessions. A low table for eating is usually the only other visible item in the main room. Chairs are only for foreigners, so they are seldom found in village homes. Tableware is equally simple. A large bowl holds the steaming rice, a slightly smaller one is filled with the spiced *hin* (a vegetable or meat stew known to Europeans as curry), and little dishes offer various condiments. These are placed in the center of the table. Each person has a plate and a small bowl filled with water but no spoon, knife, or fork. The only spoons are for serving the rice and *hin*.

The men of the family eat first, sitting cross-legged at the low table. Each person spoons rice, *hin*, a dab of the fermented shrimp paste called *nga-pi*, plus various other condiments onto his plate, then eats, using his fingers in a prescribed and very neat manner. A plate of fruit concludes the meal. Hands are washed before the meal, and fingers are rinsed in the small bowls of water at the end. Then the women and younger children repeat the whole process.

Most of the household possessions are related to cooking. An iron brazier or a small brick fireplace with a grill supports the cooking pots above the glowing charcoal. That same charcoal fire provides welcome warmth on chilly mornings during the cool months. This requires no extra work, as fresh rice is cooked each morning and served with hot tea.

Clay pots of various sizes are used for both storage and cooking. Most will have tight-fitting lids. One, perhaps three feet tall, will be filled daily with fresh water from the village well or a nearby stream; they are slightly porous, and the slow evaporation keeps the water remarkably cool. Another large jar holds rice, and smaller ones hold good cooking oil, honey, *jaggery* sugar, candied ginger, and the ubiquitous *nga-pi*, a fermented paste made from prawns. Onions, herbs, and various spices hang from the rafters or grow in the garden until needed to prepare the meal.

Part of every housewife's day is the long, tedious grinding of the condiments. Chili, turmeric, cumin, and the other ingredients must be ground into powder and mixed to make curry seasoning. For this, the housewife owns a good grinding stone and both a small and large mortar and pestle. The latter is used to make rice flour for cakes and delicacies. And, of course, the wife will have assorted sharp kitchen *dahs* for cutting, spoons or paddles for stirring, and clay or iron pans and pots for cooking. These everyday items are often mentioned in the folk tales.

Cleanliness and Clothing

There is no "bathroom" in the Western sense, yet the Burmese have a long tradition of personal cleanliness—and the hot climate makes frequent bathing a pleasure as well as a social courtesy. This is accomplished using the centuries-old skill of remaining private while bathing in public, either at the village well, the nearest stream, or on the family veranda. And it is the traditional *longyi*, or skirt, worn by both sexes that makes this possible.

A *longyi* is a simple tube made by stitching together the cut ends of a piece of cloth about two yards long and one yard wide, which is pulled over the head and folded to fit the particular wearer. Women make a deep fold in front, securing this flat, smooth "pleat" at the waist, while men tie the extra material into a pouch-like bunch.

For bathing, this skirt forms a private "cabana." At the village well, the young woman pulls her longyi up beneath her bodice and blouse, retying it just above her breasts. She then removes these upper clothes, pours water over herself and soaps as though the skirt were part of her skin. Then, after rinsing herself with more water, she sits to visit with her friends while the air dries her.

Then, holding her damp longyi in her teeth, she deftly maneuvers herself into the clean clothes she brought with her. Even young girls are already skillful at this. Men also bathe at the village well, but most boys just splash naked in a nearby stream.

At home, bathing is much the same, standing on the front or back veranda, using a basin and pitchers of water. Damp clothes that are to be worn again are hung to dry over a line strung the length of the large family room, and clothes that require washing will later be taken to the nearest stream, soaped, and thrashed against the rocks.

The family latrine is usually a pit in a corner of the garden, made semi-private with plants and hedges or perhaps a fence a few feet high. A couple of boards make a platform for the feet and a jar of water serves in place of toilet paper. Some town families do have indoor toilet and bathing facilities. These usually consist of a commode (which a servant must empty and clean daily), a large earthen jar of water, and a dipper. The bather stands on a wooden grate over a concrete slab that has a channel for draining away the water. He dips water over himself, soaps, then pours more water for rinsing.

Traditional Burmese clothing is simple, useful, modest and very attractive. A man in his best silk *longyi*, Burmese style shirt, and shantung jacket, wearing a jaunty silk *gaungbaung* (turban) on his head—is an elegant sight, and many prefer these traditional clothes, especially for important occasions. Women generally wear a brightly-colored cotton *longyi* for household tasks, but, at least until the disruptions that began with World War II, most owned several excellent silk ones for "best"—an excursion to the pagoda, errands about town, or visiting friends and relatives.

A woman's blouse, called an *aingyi* (ain-gee), is usually white cotton cloth, muslin or percale for everyday, batiste or sheer silk for dressy occasions. This waist-length blouse is cut in a simple flat "T" shape. Sleeves may be long or short, but always long for dressy occasions. It is collarless, opens down the front with a placket, and has cloth loops for attaching the ornaments used as buttons.

Most women have several sets of these removable buttons which they change to compliment whatever *longyi* they are wearing that day. These ornaments are beads of faceted colored glass (or precious gems) attached to a small ring of silver. This ring is first slipped through the cloth loop on one side, then the opposing loop, closing the blouse. Under this blouse, a woman wears a cotton bodice trimmed with lace. It serves as both bra and slip. As a result, even in an extremely sheer aingyi, the woman looks modest and neat.

When a woman dresses up she will add a number of other accessories—including gold or silver necklaces, bracelets and *nagats* (ear studs set with real gems such as ruby, sapphire, or diamond). Even for her daily tasks, she makes a neat bun of her hair, but for a special occasion she will wind it into an intricate *sedon* fastened with combs and ornamented with fresh flowers. Her preferred cosmetic is a cream-colored paste called *thanaka* made from powdered boxwood. She smooths this cooling and slightly astringent paste on her cheeks and forehead, leaving whitish patches.

Now she adds a long narrow scarf of matching chiffon painted with flowers and butterflies. Her thong slippers (*pahnats*) are made of reed or wood, covered with velvet, and also painted with tiny flowers. Ready at last, she will pick up one of her bamboo parasols and start down the dusty road. Perhaps today she chooses a parasol covered with orange silk. Like her scarf and slippers, it too is painted with flowers and butterflies. With intense sunshine pouring from the sky, a parasol is more than an attractive accessory: it is a necessity.

Indeed the umbrella is almost a national emblem. A white silk umbrella over the throne is the symbol of royalty. Pagodas are topped with an umbrella cap or *hti* of lacy gilded ironwork. This is often gem-studded and fringed with little bells that tinkle in the breeze. Monks carry huge umbrellas almost six feet across, and an elderly abbot will have a young novice who walks beside him carrying the large shade to protect the revered shaved head. There are large black umbrellas of oiled silk for everyday use, and roadside vendors open extra-large ones as a canopy over their stalls.

In the past, virtually everyone in Burma carried an umbrella, but today more and more of the younger people go bareheaded or wear cloth hats. With three to four months of drenching rain, and six or seven of punishing sun, umbrellas are immensely useful, and like everything else in Burman life, their design combines beauty and practicality.

For really special occasions, court dress—jackets with gold sashes and stiff turned up "wings," extra long longyis and golden, pagoda-shaped crowns—comes out of the clothing chests of the wealthy and kin of former royals. But such clothing is not really appropriate to the climate, and its gilded ornateness lacks the simple beauty of Burma's traditional dress.

Daily Rice

In the past, rice farming was a combination of individual ownership and family cooperation. The farmer owned his field, his house, and its lot, and was responsible for these. The crop was his to sell, the money or barter his to keep. But as villages were mostly made up of aunts, uncles, and cousins, these extended families worked in cooperation during part of the planting and harvest time. Current reports are unclear as to who owns what today, or to what extent tractors plow or machines reap, but the stories in this volume reflect patterns of life that have existed for millennia, so we will "time travel" back a century or so to picture rice farming as it once existed.

Once the rains begin, it is time to prepare. The farmer's paddy field is usually a considerable distance from his house. He walks through the pouring rain, hitches the heavy wooden plow behind his buffalo, and urges the great gray beast forward through the thick muck. In a few days the village women and girls come with baskets of young paddy plants. They wade calf-deep in the flooded field moving in concert; they bend, press a young plant into the mud, stand, and bend again.

Row after row, field after field, day after day they continue this backbreaking work until, in every dike-bordered field, tender stalks wave above the gray-blue water.

In the next few months, farmers pull away unwanted weeds and channel water from the river when fields become too dry, using irrigation techniques dating back at least a thousand years. Gradually the skies become cloudless and the sun ripens the paddy to a tawny gold. Once again, a whole village works together. Sharp sickles cut the sheaves, which are then taken to a large flat threshing stone or platform.

Several women, working as a team, beat the sheaves against the stone to free the rice grains. In large mortars, other women pound these just enough to loosen the husk.

This rough-milled rice is spread on mats and raked to allow the sun to dry each kernel. In a day or two it will be winnowed. Dry paddy is placed on a shallow bamboo tray about a yard across, then flipped into the air, allowing the breeze to carry away the chaff. This is repeated until only firm brown kernels remain. However, as most Burmese prefer white rice, the woman of the house now grinds the rice further on her millstone, or perhaps takes it to a nearby miller.

The Market: A Display of Crafts and Skills

It is in the bazaar that Burma's wide range of crafts and skills becomes apparent. And here Burma's women display their initiative and independence most clearly.

Well before dawn, people stream from the villages, baskets and jars balanced on heads, infants strapped to backs. Men shoulder panniers—balancing heavy jars filled with honey or palm oil—or bamboo baskets loaded with watermelon or mangoes. At the market, they will unroll their mats and arrange their wares, placing hot red chilies next to fresh green vegetables and waxy amber, russet, and golden fruits. Between the intensely busy period of rice planting and harvesting, the farm families have been growing or gathering these other "fruits" of the land.

For most of Burma, market day is periodical—once a week or perhaps every five days—and it may be held in different towns or villages on a rotating basis. Vendors travel up to fifteen miles. By sunrise, the market is bustling and noisy with a holiday atmosphere. Women laugh and joke with each other, asking after the well-being of families. Many a customer is the vendor from a few stalls away. People buy and sell, using simple pan balances and brass weights. They paid in rupees and annas in British Colonial days, and use kyats today.

One man sells sweet juicy sugar cane. A woman displays the neatly rolled cigars, cheroots, and *salays* (extra long white cigars smoked mostly by women) she has been making at home all week. A girl, scarcely ten, sells the silk her sister has woven on a large foot loom at home. The child also sells bracelets and other finery on concession from the town silversmith, who knows her mother and likes the child's meticulous honesty. Besides, everyone knows the mother sits only a few stalls away selling flowers, root and all, kept moist in plantain leaves.

Finery sold at the bazaar is set with semi-precious stones: amethyst, garnet, spinel, mother of pearl, or second quality jade. And much of what is sold is only colored glass. The "royal" gems: ruby, sapphire, emerald, fine jade from Burma's mountains, and pearls from her surrounding seas, are too valuable to be sold in a market stall. These are bought and sold by goldsmiths whose workshops in the cities and larger towns are barred and guarded.

Fans of carved ivory or brightly dyed feathers are spread like a courting peacock. These are displayed beside ace-shaped fans woven from fine strands of bamboo. Long narrow scarves of pastel chiffon, decorated with painted flowers and butterflies, are arranged into a rainbow next to *gaungbaungs* of wicker and silk. "Leprosy charm" bracelets of mother-of-pearl and silver nest in a small cardboard box beside a row of intricately carved ivory letter openers, ivory and tortoise-shell combs, and shiny red hollow seeds, slightly smaller than an orange pit. Each of these seeds contains a tiny ivory elephant—sometimes many, all sealed in with an ivory stopper—a miniature wonder destined to become some child's special treasure.

A bee-keeper offers jars of honey. Next to him an old man sells the *jaggery*, palm oil, and liquor he and his sons have processed from toddy palm trees. Alcohol drinking is frowned on by the Buddhist monks, and the folk tales scoff at the drunkard or the "opium-eater," as addicts are called. With typical humor, though, many Burmese tales allow these fools to best their ghost or ogre opponents—just by sheer dumb luck.

At another stall, a woman sells parasols made in a workshop in Kemendine. There, teams of women work together, some making handles, others the spokes or the silk coverings, while still others assemble, decorate or varnish. Umbrella making is also a cottage industry, in which one woman, alone or with her daughters, completes the entire process. The parasol vendor also sells *pah-nats* (thong slippers). To make these, reeds are wound and sewn to form a sturdy but slightly flexible sole to which thong straps are attached. These are then covered with dark cotton velvet and finally decorated with dabs of paint to resemble flowers.

Woven bamboo baskets of all shapes and sizes, work hats, mats, and exquisite little boxes to hold such treasures as silver neck chains, *aingyi* buttons, or a woman's best *nagats* are hand-crafted both in homes and workshops.

Much of the silk or checked cotton used to make the essential *longyi* is (or was) also woven at home on large foot looms. Women sew the cotton batiste *aingyis*, hand-stitching tiny neat seams, or perhaps using an ancient Singer sewing machine. Other women tat lace to trim the cotton bodices, or specialize in embroidery, making handkerchiefs, elaborate cut-work tea cloths, or the "royal" costumes, gaudy with gold thread and shiny beads, needed by the troupe of actors and dancers who will perform next week's *pwé* (open air opera).

From Prome and Pagan fine lacquerware has arrived. It is sold all week long in a merchant's small shop along the main street of the town, but on market day the shop owner has a young assistant take a cartload of his wares to a stall he uses each week.

This craft, developed in China at least 1,000 B.C., arrived in the Mon kingdom of Thaton by the first century A.D. and was brought to Pagan when Anawrahta Min captured Thaton in A.D. 1057. Individual families living in Prome or on the outskirts of the ancient ruins of Pagan preserve this skilled craft, training sons and daughters who serve as apprentices and do the many preliminary steps before father, the master craftsman, completes the layered, scratched, and gilded designs. The best lacquerware has a light core, either of bamboo wicker or horsehair, creating a bowl or box that can be flexed without cracking. Cheaper pieces use a lathed wooden core and fewer layers of the precious sap.

While Burma's kings still ruled, many skilled artisans lived near the royal cities, producing the luxuries appropriate to the exalted "Descendant of the Sun." Today Mandalay remains the center for most of these specialized skills, but the artisan's patron is now the tourist, the visitor, the former British colonial, the American missionary who desires a beautiful memento, or even a local businessman who admires these echoes of royalty.

The silversmith still makes a fine *repoussé* silver bowl with its mixture of high and low relief, its scenes of royal elephants, temples, processions, pagodas, and nats. But such a bowl can take up to six months to create and requires a large weight of silver. Kings once rewarded a silversmith well for these fine bowls, or for silver daggers and sheaths, serving trays, betel boxes, medallions, and ornaments.

Today, few can pay a fair price for such items, so more and more frequently this work is turned out by apprentices. It is still very expensive and still worth the price asked, but lacks the exceptional artistry of work by a master craftsman.

Teak woodcarving, also done mostly for royalty in the past, included intricately carved teak wall panels, chests, trays, altar brackets, pictorial plaques, and stylized elephants supporting brass gongs. Perhaps because wood is much less expensive than silver, a number of gifted carvers still support themselves with their old craft.

While these exceptional woodcarvers are usually men working alone, it is women in workshops who turn out the hundreds of wooden statues of nats painted in bright colors, or make "Buddha in a bottle" souvenirs—carving, gilding—and fitting each piece into place in the narrow-necked bottles.

Several vendors display small alabaster Buddhas, six or seven inches high. Many of these come from one or two villages located near Burma's alabaster quarries. There, almost the whole village works together to produce hundreds of these stylized images, large and small. Men rough chisel, and women sculpt and polish row upon row of benignly smiling Buddhas. Unfortunately, few of these villagers have any particular talent for carving.

There may be incense (joss) sticks or small booklets of gold leaf on sale here as well as at the pagodas. Most of Burma's gold leaf is produced in workshops where each of about a dozen women does one step, from purchasing the gold to pounding it into thinner and thinner pieces. The final sheets are so thin, they must be laid between small squares of oiled bamboo paper. These are then bound into little booklets and sold to the devout, who lavish yet more layers of gold on their revered pagodas and images.

A potter sits on a mat shaping small bowls as his foot-treadle sets the wheel spinning. Vendors sell earthenware of all types and sizes. Wherever the rivers yield good clay, a potter probably lives nearby, but in the Irrawaddy delta several villages specialize in turning out hundreds of pots, particularly the large water jars or *chattees*, some as tall as four feet.

The smell of fish wafts by—dried and salted or caught fresh during the night by the fishermen, whose wares are eagerly purchased, even though these men are despised for taking life. A meal of rice is not complete without the fermented prawn paste called *nga-pi*.

Live chickens, trussed together by their feet, rest under a wicker dome. The vendor, probably a Hindu or Muslim, will "dispatch" the bird if the buyer wishes. This allows the demerit of taking life to fall onto this unfortunate and presumably inferior person, the vendor, rather than on the family who cooks and eats the flesh.

A few stalls away, a table is piled with gardenia, frangipani, orchids, cosmos, and canna lilies, flooding the air with fragrance A glass blower surrounded by wide-eyed children is creating tiny creatures of colored glass. A black cauldron steams with the mouth-watering smells of rice-flour pancakes soaked with honey or topped with chives and spices. A woman buys several of these pancakes, which are handed to her wrapped in plantain leaves.

The soft, haunting sound of a bamboo flute insinuates itself through the chatter and bustle, quickly drawing an audience, mostly of children. The onlookers watch intently as a man picks up a narrow length of reed and begins to burn holes into its sides, using an iron poker that has been heating in a tray of glowing charcoal. Behind him are drums of all sorts, a Burmese harp shaped like the harp of David, bamboo clappers, and a Burmese xylophone. This itinerant flute-maker has been traveling from market to market selling his flutes. He has many eager customers, especially young boys with a few coins, many of whom become very skillful at playing the pentatonic melodies.

Another stall displays wares from the hill people. The Shan weave handsome, sturdy, and spacious shoulder bags with brightly colored string on fine black cotton warp. Next to these is an excellent array of fine steel *dahs* from the Chin hills. These knives are sought for the skilled smithing and their distinctive wood and reed sheaths. The vendor is probably one of the many boatmen who work for the merchant owners of boats and rafts that carry rice down the river to the delta. In the folk tales these "country bumpkins" often give a greedy, bigoted boat owner his comeuppance.

Traditional wares such as these described above have been found in Burma's bazaars for centuries, but more and more, imports are also found: watches, radios, cassette players, tins of sardines, baseball caps, floppy cloth hats, sunglasses, and jeans—especially jeans.

By mid-morning, much of the buying and selling is completed, though most of the vendors, predominantly women, will stay until late afternoon for the sake of foreigners and latecomers. They welcome the quieter pace, drinking tea and chatting quietly over noon meals of rice brought from home in tiffin lunch cans. Then, at about four o'clock, they will pack what little remains unsold plus their day's purchases and any money they did not spend and start the long walk back home.

A Woman's Place

In Burma, a woman's place is in the home, the garden, or the rice field—weaving silk or baskets, rolling cigars for the next market day, cooking for her family, washing clothes in the river, bearing, raising, and teaching her children.

A woman's place is also in hundreds of workshops where she is paid per piece for her skill at making parasols or slippers, or beating gold thinner than tissue. An older women or widow might become a broker, matching merchants who have commodities or land to sell with other merchants who wish to purchase these, or she might be a matchmaker arranging suitable marriages— though more young people are choosing their own partners today.

Today, a woman might become an editor in a small publishing firm in Rangoon or Mandalay, a teacher, a nurse, a doctor. Perhaps, one day, a woman will become president.

Even after Buddhism became the dominant religion in Burma, bringing overtones of the Indian view that women are lesser creatures, the centuries of prior attitudes did not vanish. Yes, a woman and her children bow to the husband, lord of the house. She serves him his meal before feeding herself. But beyond these few stylized courtesies, she remains her own person.

Marriage is neither a legal nor a religious bond. It is a formalized announcement to the community that two have joined. And the ceremony itself can be as simple as having a parent join the couple's hands with a thread, offer a plate of rice from which both eat, or present a silver bowl filled with water into which each prospective partner plunges a hand.

Several *pongyis* (Buddhist monks), including the *Sayadaw* (abbot), might be invited to read or chant from the scriptures. Indeed the *Sayadaw* might ask the couple the traditional questions about each partner's willingness to join in marriage. But a beloved uncle or older friend can perform this role instead.

For the wealthy, the groom will arrive at the bride's home on a white pony led by a good friend. Both men will be dressed very grandly with *longyis* of excellent silk, perhaps a *tussoré* poplin jacket, and their best *gaungbaung*... But the bride will outshine them both. She will emerge from her dressing room also dressed in a fine *longyi*, a sheer, long-sleeved *aingyi*, and a long chiffon scarf draped from her neck. She will also be adorned with dozens of gold and silver bracelets and necklaces, many set with real gems. Her hair, literally her "crowning glory" is combed into a satiny black *sedon* (resembling a top-hat sans the brim) and festooned with a cascading spray of jasmine and tiny rose buds. One long, curling lock is pulled loose and allowed to tumble to her shoulder. Her face is a work of art. Her eyebrows form a perfect thin semi-circle like those on *nat* or Buddha images. Her eyes are accented in black, and her lips and cheeks are rouged.

The couple kneel on large silk-covered cushions before a presiding elder. Two cone-shaped bouquets have been placed on small pillows before them. Holding the flowers between their palms in a prayerful positions, the bride and groom listen to the blessings, speak their assent and join hands in the symbol of union.

After this ceremony, the solemn mood changes back into one of celebration. Everyone congratulates the couple, feasts on delicacies, and receives a gift. There may even be a *pwé* to attend, arranged and paid for by the bride's parents.

In a more modest wedding, the groom will walk to the bride's house with a special friend. The women of the family will pass around plates of special sweets and cakes, and again there will be gifts for all, perhaps a fine be-ribboned cigar. Guests do not bring gifts; they receive them. But of course, the families will have done what they can to help the couple set up housekeeping.

After the festivities are over, the young bride and groom walk together to their new house. That is honeymoon enough!

In marriage, the woman does not change her name (there is no such thing as a "family name"). By tradition, whatever the woman earns is hers—to share with the family or not as she chooses. Whatever wealth she had before the marriage, or earns after, is hers to keep even if the marriage falls apart. Should she find her husband lazy or intolerable, she has only to repeat three times that he is no longer welcome in her home.

Still, divorce is not widespread and physical abuse of any kind is rare within families. Children are seldom hit. Nor are they shamed. The parents guide in much the same way Western parents treat their infants—that is, attracting the child's attention to something acceptable, presenting him or her with a very small list of "no's," and consistently demonstrating courtesy and consideration in their own behavior. Above all, the Burman never strikes the head or face! That is the supreme insult.

In Burma as elsewhere, cruel behavior surfaces from

somewhere deep in the universal human psyche. Burma has its share of *dacoits* (bandits) and cut-throats, its desperate villains, its slothful, and its addicts. It has its vicious soldiers and callous generals and unscrupulous men seeking to gain or maintain power. Still, the gentle, affectionate approach to child-rearing may be responsible for the good-natured, laughter-loving, and hospitable national character on which so many visitors have remarked.

The Holy Life: Gaining Merit

On a hilltop not far from the village, a white pagoda gleams softly in the moonlight. The occasional screech of a nighthawk, the sudden tock-tock of a house lizard, the constant thrumming of cicadas, and a shiver of pagoda bells punctuate the hours just before dawn. Suddenly, as the sun rises, a deep-throated gong shatters the stillness, followed by a chorus of wooden clappers. The monks of the nearby *pongyi kyang* (monastery) are awaking.

The monks will wash, say their morning prayers, and set out with their black lacquer *thabeits*—alms or begging bowls. The orange-robed *pongyis* will leave the monastery, walking silently in single file, their eyes fixed on a point just a few feet before them. As they pass through the village, women will hurry out of the houses to add a spoonful of rice, or a sweet pancake to each offered bowl.

The monks do not look at the givers nor do they thank them. It is the monks who have done the favor, giving the women the opportunity to earn merit by their act of charity. Even when a novice is the woman's own young son of nine or ten, she should avoid speaking to him, and if she must she will using his new Pali or religious name.

When the *pongyis* return to the monastery, they will eat and go to their appointed duties, some to learn, some to teach, some to read and memorize the holy words. Soon the village boys come running to the monastery. They will seat themselves on the floor and begin to scratch letters on their slate boards or read aloud from their primers. Their teacher walks among them, frowning if a child falls silent, smiling when he chants at the top of his lungs.

During a rest from lessons, the village boys climb trees, play a mumbledy-peg type of game with their knives, toss pebbles or large smooth tamarind beans at a target, or practice kicking their wicker *chinlon* balls. The young novices are supposed to be too serious now for such games, but they usually manage some childish fun anyway.

Before noon, the village boys leave and the monks eat their second and last meal of the day, a small one. From then until the next morning they will fast and meditate.

Meanwhile the grounds of both the monastery and the pagoda will be swept and cleaned by a group of women, the "pagoda slaves." These women are not from the Burmese farm villages; they live in a village of their own. Their grandparents or great-grandparents were captured in battle many years before and were given by the king to the pagoda en masse, as his gift, one that earned him much merit.

For many years there has been nothing to keep these women doing this daily service except their own belief that it is their duty, and perhaps a superstitious fear that the ancient curse might be true. Any slave who left or shirked her duty presumably suffered terrible misfortune both for herself and her family.

The monastery itself, unlike the simple village houses, is built of handsomely carved teak and has a multi-tiered roof with ornate upturned corners. Its veranda and main floor are raised only a few feet above the ground and the front room is mostly open. This allows a villager to speak with the *Sayadaw* (abbot) while he kneels on the veranda. Out of respect, the supplicant's head must remain lower than that of the seated *Shin* (Reverend).

These holy men are monks, not priests. They advise, they teach, they hold considerable power politically, but they do not administer any sort of sacrament. Curiously, most astrologers are also monks, or *pônnas*. Like the ubiquitous *nat* worship, Burmese Buddhism was never able to shake off a strong reliance on numerology, astrology, or other divinations. After a baby is born, one of the parents' first acts will be to take a record of the exact hour and day of the birth to the monastery. The astrologer will use this information to prepare a chart that will guide the child throughout his life in choosing auspicious dates and places for his endeavors.

Indeed the influence of the stars is so strongly believed that a person's name is based on his birth day, with certain initials for the days of the week. When that person goes to the pagoda he will stop at the appropriate planetary post to light a candle or circle it respectfully.

Shin-Pyu: Becoming a Dignified Human

About the age of nine or ten, virtually every boy from a devout Buddhist family will go through a ritual called *shin-pyu*—"becoming a dignified human." It is probably the most important moment in his life. This is his initiation into the "brotherhood of monks" as a novice disciple of the "Great Teacher." It marks his departure from a nearly uninhibited boyhood. Whether he remains in the monastery a few days, a few weeks, or a whole lifetime, he will never again be a carefree child.

Often boys from several families are initiated at the same time in order to share the cost of the festivities that usually accompany such a celebration. For weeks before the ceremony, the boy will be instructed in a catechism of the basic tenants of Theravada Buddhist belief, in the Pali words of scripture he will have to recite, and in every move and behavior that will be expected of him as a novice.

Finally the anticipated day arrives.

In a recreation of the story of Prince Siddhartha Gautama, the fourth Buddha of the present epoch, the initiate is dressed in the ancient royal styles of India and Burma. His clothes will be the finest and most elaborate his family can afford, with all the gold and silver chains, bracelets, jewels, rings, even a crownlike turban his family can gather, borrow, or rent. He will ride to the monastery on a pony, or be carried in a sedan chair, for as a royal prince, his feet must not touch the earth. Musicians are hired to play as his procession passes.

Early that morning the women of his family will take an elaborate feast to the monastery. First all the monks are served, then the male guests and last the women. When the "prince" arrives he must prostrate himself three times to the monks and ask, in Pali, to be admitted to the brotherhood, vowing to follow its rules.

Now all his finery and royal clothes are removed, and he is left in a simple *longyi* and shirt. Next, his head is shaved and he is given the eight things a monk requires: three robes (the monks will dress him), a belt, a razor, a needle (for mending), a strainer (to prevent him from accidentally swallowing a living thing), a fan (to hide the temptation of women from his eyes), an umbrella (to shade his head), and his alms bowl. When this last item is hung over his shoulder, the child has become a novice member of the Buddha's disciples.

The ceremony is intended to impress on the boy's young mind the major lesson of the Buddha—wealth and power mean nothing; only right thought and right living are important. To covet the luxuries of life is to distract the mind from the true path.

Unlike churches, synagogues, or mosques, pagodas are not places where congregations meet. They are intended to invite meditation and solitary reverence. The stupa (cone shaped monument) often encloses a sacred relic: a hair, tooth, splinter of bone or some ash, reputedly from the Buddha's body.

Pagodas vary in shape and size, many showing their Indian origins, but most resemble a huge bell. The stupa and its square platform are built of brick, plastered smooth, and washed with white lime. Some stupas are then covered with tissue-thin layers of gold, which often builds over the years into a considerable thickness. All are crowned with a *hti*, the sacred golden umbrella.

Each pagoda will have a Buddha image framed in a niche, and an altar for placing flowers, incense (joss) sticks, and other offerings. *Chinthe* (crested lion-dogs) will guard the entrance, most will also have astrological posts and even *nat* images.

Some pagodas are temples, in that they have interior corridors with additional shrines, pictures, and other sacred objects. For example, the magnificent Ananda Temple in Pagan, built by Kyanzittha Min in A.D.1091, contains a series of glazed tiles picturing some of the most beloved Jataka tales, stories believed to tell of the Buddha's earlier lives.

The Payartaga

Building a pagoda is one of the highest acts of merit a devout Buddhist can perform. Of course the wealthy Burman does not build the pagoda with his own hands, but he does devote much of his wealth to pay the cost of its construction. He will buy as many precious stones as he can afford and will try to find a suitable relic to place in its core. Even with no relic, a valuable ruby or emerald dedicated to the honor of the Buddha and entombed in the stupa will create a sacred shrine or *payar*.

From that day on the donor will be entitled to call himself a *Payartaga* (pagoda builder). The title is highly respected and brings the knowledge that this man has earned great merit, absolving many past misdeeds. If, however, the payartaga has devotedly followed the Buddha's eight-fold path, the added merit should assure his rebirth to a much higher level— perhaps even as a *nat* or a blessed spirit.

A more modest act of merit is to build a *zayat* or rest house. In a village of any size there is certain to be at least one where travelers may sleep without charge. These rest houses often consist of one large room, sometimes with no walls—only a wooden floor a few feet above the ground, a hearth and a roof. There the traveler can spread his sleeping mat, cook his pot of rice, and boil water for his tea, sheltered from rain and resting safely above the creatures of the night. But many *zayats* have the reputation of being haunted by ghosts or ogres, and are certainly the frequent refuge of the drunkard or opium addict regularly turned away from his or any other house. This combination makes for jolly stories that set everyone laughing at the incredible luck of the fool who bests the malevolent spirits.

A Final Note

As mentioned in the beginning, the stories are paradoxical because the people are paradoxical. Their beliefs and customs have accumulated like layers of an onion. But at the core, beneath the changes of the last millennium, they remain basically the same egalitarian people who left the high plateaus of Tibet and Central Asia. They remain a people who love to laugh, who do not worry overmuch if the villain does not get his "comeuppance" in this lifetime, and who settle disputes by seeking the advice of an arbiter.

They are a people who keep decorum and modesty in their daily lives without prudery, give their women uncommon equality and respect, and who especially admire a clever protagonist, be he villain or hero.

All these paradoxes appear in the stories—stories intended for listeners of every age—stories intended to entertain, to preserve the culture, to instruct, and to strengthen the bonds between the generations.

Part I: Tales of Wonder and Romance

The Storyteller

full moon rises above the black wall of jungle—silhouetting palms, bamboos, and the sturdy stilt houses of the village. The light of the moon outlines the bell-shaped spire of a nearby pagoda and accents the crested heads of the pagoda's two enormous *chinthe* guardians. This is a special night. The old Storyteller has come to the village.

All day whispers and giggles of anticipation have punctuated the daily chores, and now the time of magic has finally arrived. Lamplight glows softly from windows, and fireflies flicker over rice-paddy fields. Water buffalo, safe in their night pens, grow silent, and under the bamboo houses, jungle fowl scratch a dust bed, cluck and chuck a few more times, and settle down to sleep.

High in the jungle trees, shrieks of magpie and lorikeet and the chatterings of the ever-excited monkeys cease at last. Instead, night peepers, crickets, and an owl are heard, and in the distance, the cry of a lonely jackal.

Now, at last, perched cross-legged on a platform in the center of the village, the old storyteller begins:

"Listen, oh my children, to the tale of the storyteller; to the strange adventure of Mong Byan, mighty hunter of Pegu. In the olden days..."

Around him cluster wide-eyed children, weary mothers, tired fathers, and wise old grandmothers, nodding at each well-remembered detail. Even youths, brimming with new loves, new hopes and age-old dreams, listen eagerly.

The old storyteller will stay a night or two as guest in one of the village homes and then walk on to the next village where he is again eagerly welcomed.

Mistress Beloved
(Ma Chit Su)

This romantic story from Burma echoes some of the elements of Cinderella and several other fairy stories with which Westerners are familiar. It also contains a streak of cannibalistic horror, more startling because the story is unfamiliar. We usually read Hansel and Gretel without a blink. In the original translation, the heroine is named Mistress Youngest, and no other character has a name. For this retelling, Ma Chit Su (Mistress Beloved) and Ma Ga Hsoh (Mistress Bother) seemed to suit.

Part One: The Sea Turtle

There was once an old fisherman and his wife who lived in a small hut by the sea. Each dawn, the two set out in their sampan to catch fish to sell at the market. Each evening, the wife would cook a meal of rice with fish curry. And each night, before she slept, the wife would light one candle to the Buddha and a second one to Thagya Min, King of the Nats, to ask for the blessing of a child.

At last, the wife gave birth to a beautiful child whom she named Ma Chit Su, meaning Mistress Beloved. The overjoyed old woman thanked the Buddha and all the spirits, and asked their protection for her child. The old fisherman, however, only grumbled that now he must feed three mouths instead of two.

Ignoring his complaints, the old woman lavished her child with love and tenderness, so not surprisingly, Ma Chit Su grew into a beautiful young woman with a loving and gentle nature. One day, the old couple went out to fish as usual. For weeks the sea had offered little for the three to sell or eat, and this day began as before. Each time they pulled in the net, it was empty. At last, near sunset, the couple pulled in a fine plump fish. The old fisherman rubbed his stomach in anticipation. But the wife cried out, "This fish is not for sale. Our daughter has become thin and pale from hunger. I claim this fish for Ma Chit Su."

Of course, a husband must obey a wife's claim, so the old man simply growled under his breath and held his peace.

After a time, they again pulled in their net. Once more it held a fish even fatter and more beautiful. Again the wife cried out, "This fish is not for sale. I claim it for Ma Chit Su."

"Old woman, you are mad," shouted the angry fisherman, and he flailed his oar, striking his wife and knocking her into the sea. She raised her arms, pleading for help, but he ignored her and rowed for shore. There he sold the two fine fish for many coins, which he promptly spent on toddy wine.

When the tavern keeper inquired about the old woman, the fisherman merely said she had fallen into the sea, and soon the village gossips spread news of the old wife's unfortunate accident. Kindly neighbors brought cakes and rice to comfort the old fisherman and his daughter.

Poor Ma Chit Su. She wept bitterly to hear of her mother's death. Each day she went about her daily chores. Each night she lit one candle to the Buddha, and another to Thagya Min, asking them to protect her mother's spirit.

After a time, the old fisherman married a wealthy widow from a nearby village who had an ugly daughter called Ma Ga Hsoh, or Mistress Bother. Perhaps, the girl's face would not have been so unpleasant had it not been soured with frowns and bad temper, and pocked with boils she picked at constantly.

The widow, Daw Hla Doke, and her daughter were much despised in their own village, for the widow's wealth had come from conniving and cheating. However, the two were well skilled at hiding their evil natures under polite gestures and false kindness, so the old fisherman suspected nothing. He was simply pleased to have found a wealthy wife, for now he could spend his days in the tavern, drinking and playing at dominoes.

After the marriage, the stepmother and her daughter promptly returned to their evil ways. They were jealous of Ma Chit Su's beauty and kind nature and delighted in causing her pain. They compelled Ma Chit Su to do all the cooking and washing and gardening, while they went daily to the bazaar to buy fine silk *longyis* and delicate silver chains. Ma Chit Su never complained, as she did not wish to burden her father, but under her smiles, her heart was breaking.

One day, after all the chores were finished, Ma Chit Su went to the edge of the sea where she sat, weeping bitterly. "Oh my beloved mother," she sobbed, "if only I could embrace you once again!"

As she gazed out over the water, an old sea turtle came swimming up. To Ma Chit Su's astonishment the turtle was also weeping. Guessing that by some miracle, this was really her own dear mother, the girl scooped the old turtle into her arms, holding the creature tenderly and speaking softly to it.

The turtle seemed so content to be with her, that Ma Chit Su felt certain this was indeed her mother. From then on, Ma Chit Su went to the shore each afternoon, where the two shared many happy hours together.

After a time, the stepmother and her daughter, noticed that Ma Chit Su seemed strangely content in spite of their evil treatment. Curious, they followed her one afternoon, and found her sitting by the sea, talking quietly to the turtle.

"We must destroy that turtle," the furious stepmother hissed to her daughter, for she, too, guessed who the turtle might be. "I will find a way!" she promised.

The next morning, Daw Hla Doke sent Ma Chit Su to the bazaar to buy rice. As soon as the girl had gone, the stepmother fried a large number of crisp rice cakes, spread them under her mattress, and lay down, pretending to be very ill.

When Ma Chit Su returned, the kind-hearted girl brought cool water for her stepmother to sip, and heated steaming cloths to sooth her brow. All this time the wicked woman lay still and appeared faint. But as soon as the husband returned from the tavern, Daw Hla Doke began turning this way and that, causing the cakes to crackle. In a loud moan she began chanting:

This side I turn, crackle, crackle.
That side I turn, crackle, crackle.
I die of splintered bones.

The worried husband immediately sent for the village physician, whom the stepmother had bribed the night before, arranging what he was to say.

The physician examined his patient, declaring there was only one cure for such a dangerous illness. Daw Hla Doke must immediately have a broth of sea turtle with plenty of turtle meat in it.

"What good fortune," cried the evil woman. "My daughter tells me a large turtle was seen near the shore just yesterday. Go, husband! Catch it at once!"

"Oh!" cried Ma Chit Su in horror. "No, father, no! Please, do not kill that turtle. It—it has become my companion. It comes to me each afternoon!" She could not tell her father more than this, for she knew he would think her mad.

In spite of the girl's frantic pleas, the old fisherman set out at once to catch the turtle. Then Ma Chit Su was ordered to prepare it for her stepmother's dinner.

How the tears flowed down her cheek as she cut the meat, dropping each piece into the simmering pot. The work was long and difficult, for the turtle was very large indeed, and Ma Chit Su had to borrow many spare bowls from her neighbors to hold all the pieces. Soon, the good aroma of turtle stew filled the cottage. The wife jumped up suddenly from her bed, calling with joy that the smell alone had cured her.

"Rejoice, husband," she cried. "We will feast together."

Then the woman turned to Ma Chit Su with a cruel smile. "You must join us too, dear child."

"No, thank you, stepmother," replied Ma Chit Su, trying to hide her horror. "I am weary and do not feel well."

But her stepmother insisted, and Ma Chit Su was forced by good manners to appear to sip the turtle broth.

"Ma Chit Su," said the stepmother after the meal was finished. "Take some of this good turtle stew to our neighbors. They have kindly lent us their bowls. Tell them of my wonderfully restored health and say I wish them good fortune."

By now, the neighbors remained friendly with the old fisherman only for gentle Ma Chit Su's sake. They had observed the cruelty of the stepmother and her daughter and had come to despise them. But Daw Hla Doke hoped she might curry some good will by this gift of food. Obediently, the girl went from cottage to cottage, returning the bowls, now filled with the fine turtle stew. Each neighbor thanked her, but noticing her sorrow, inquired what they might do to ease her distress.

"Please," answered Ma Chit Su each time, "accept the food and enjoy it, but save the bones. Place them under the eaves just above your door. That way, I will not disturb your rest when I come for them tonight."

That night, when everyone was sleeping, Ma Chit Su slipped from her bed, gathered the turtle bones, and buried them beside the cottage door, chanting: "If I truly love my mother, may a tree with silver and gold fruit grow here to mark her grave."

The next morning, to everyone's astonishment, a tree covered with gold and silver fruit stood glittering near the door of the cottage. Neighbors came from all over the village to gasp at this wonder. Just at this time, the King, riding high on his royal hunting elephant, happened to come through the village. Noticing the crowd and the marvelous tree, he stopped to admire it and ask to whom it belonged.

"It is my daughter's tree, Your Majesty," cried the stepmother, promptly pushing Ma Ga Hsoh forward.

The king looked skeptically at the sour faced stepsister. "If this is indeed your tree, gather the fruit," he ordered. Ma Ga Hsoh immediately climbed the tree and began tugging at the fruit. She pulled and pulled, but the fruit refused to be plucked.

"I do not believe this tree belongs to you," said the King, angrily. He looked about at the crowd of neighbors. "Does anyone know the true owner?"

"Sire, I believe this tree must belong to Ma Chit Su," said a neighbor, bowing.

"Mistress Beloved?" mused the King. "What a good omen. Fetch her at once," he commanded.

Ma Chit Su came from the stream where she had been washing her stepmother's clothes. She bowed prettily when she saw the King. The moment the King saw the kindness in the maiden's face, he promptly fell in love. Nevertheless, he asked, "Does this tree belong to you, Mistress Beloved?"

"Hou'ke. Yes, Sire," Ma Chit Su replied, her head respectfully bowed.

"Then gather me some fruit," he commanded.

Ma Chit Su sat beneath the branches of the tree and chanted, "If this tree belongs to me, may all the fruits fall onto my lap." Immediately a cascade of gold and silver fruit fell from the tree.

The delighted King held out his hand to Ma Chit Su. "Will you come with me to be my Queen?" he asked. Ma Chit Su looked at the face of the King, and seeing it was both good and handsome, she agreed. The King helped Ma Chit Su climb onto his elephant, and together they rode off to the palace.

Part Two: The White Egret

The stepmother and stepsister smiled and waved and pretended to be pleased at Ma Chit Su's good fortune, but their teeth gnashed with jealousy and rage. Just as soon as the King's cortege was out of sight, the stepsister raced for an ax and furiously began chopping down the magical tree, splintering it into firewood.

"Be patient, my daughter," said the stepmother. "Ma Chit Su will suffer. I will find a way," she promised.

After some months had passed, the two evil women finally worked out a plan to kill Ma Chit Su. First, they sent a message to the palace, saying they were sorry for their past unkindness and begging Ma Chit Su to forgive them. They told her she was sorely missed and asked her to return for a few weeks' visit.

The kind-hearted Ma Chit Su immediately forgave them and promptly asked the King for permission to visit her family. As she did not wish anyone to believe her good fortune had made her self-important, she went with only a few attendants, and as soon as she arrived she sent them away, asking them to return exactly one month to the day.

The stepmother and stepsister pretended to be overjoyed at seeing Ma Chit Su once again, and acted very sorry for the way they had mistreated her in the past. For several days they continued to appear friendly and loving, while actually they were eagerly waiting for the best chance to kill her.

One morning while they were eating, Daw Hla Doke dropped a spoon, which fell through a crack in the floor. Ma Chit Su, assuming it to be an accident, went below to fetch it, but just as she bent over to retrieve the spoon, the wicked women poured a cauldron of boiling water through the crack. Instantly, Ma Chit Su was transformed into a white paddy egret who flew swiftly away.

"Well," exclaimed the annoyed stepmother, "at least, as a bird, that snippet can no longer be queen, and you, my daughter, shall go to the palace in her stead, just as we have planned."

When the court attendants returned to fetch their queen, Ma Ga Hsoh stood in the doorway dressed in the queen's fine clothes, her face partially hidden by a veil. The head steward took one look, declaring, "You are not our Queen. Who are you?"

"Oh, Aung Din," replied the stepsister, who had carefully

learned certain names beforehand, "I am indeed your Queen. A terrible illness has afflicted me these past weeks. It has disfigured me terribly and left these ugly boils on my skin."

The skeptical attendant could do nothing but take the false Queen to the palace. But when the King came to the Queen's chambers to greet her, he stared in horror. "You are not my dear wife!" he exclaimed. "Who are you?"

"Oh my King, I am your own Ma Chit Su. A terrible illness afflicted me while I was away. Do you not recognize me beneath these scars and boils?"

The King shook his head. "I cannot believe you are my beloved wife. Illness could blemish your skin, but it could not change the shape of your forehead."

"Oh, my King," replied the false Queen, "I missed you so much I wept each night, banging my head over and over against the wall, causing it to change shape."

Again the King shook his head. "No. I do not believe you. Besides, your nose is now long and ugly. My beloved Queen's was not like that at all."

"Oh, my King," the false Queen replied again, "My tears flowed so freely that I had to constantly wipe my nose. Thus it has become long and swollen."

The King still did not believe Ma Ga Hsoh, but he could not be certain, so he thought of another test. "Woman, if you are indeed my Queen, you have great skill at weaving. Weave me a new robe before morning. Only my beloved will know the patterns and colors I prefer." At this the false Queen gasped. She started to think of some excuse, but before she could speak, the King strode away.

From the palace eves, the white egret had watched all this. Ma Chit Su could not hate, and did not wish to bring about her stepsister's death by doing nothing. Further, she wished her beloved King to have the fine robe he desired, so in spite of her sorrow, she flew to the loom, took up the spindle and began to weave.

By morning an exquisite robe was finished. But as soon as the egret dropped the spindle, Ma Ga Hsoh snatched it up and hurled it, piercing the bird through the heart. Then the false Queen summoned the head cook and ordered him to roast the egret for the King's dinner.

When the King arrived, he was puzzled to see such a handsome robe. Yet he still could not believe the woman who stood before him was truly his wife. All morning he paced the halls in a state of deep gloom, puzzling and shaking his head.

At noon, when he sat to eat, a servant brought in the roasted egret. "What is this?" he demanded of the false Queen.

"It is a meddlesome paddy bird, my husband. It flew into my window last night, tangling itself among the threads on my loom and knotting them. Your robe would have been even more beautiful had it not been for that stupid bird! In anger I killed it and ordered it roasted especially for you.

Now the King was absolutely certain. This woman could not possibly be his Queen, for Ma Chit Su was gentle and could never have done such a thing. "Poor little bird," the King lamented. "I do not wish to eat you." And with that he ordered the servant to take it away.

The servant also felt sorry for the bird. Instead of eating it or giving it to his fellow servants, he slipped outside, burying it near the back gate of the palace. That next morning, a large quince tree stood at that very spot, heavy with ripe quince fruit. But only the servant could guess how it came to be there, and he did not say, as he suspected the false Queen of evil magic.

Part Three: The Fruit Maiden

Now, that very afternoon, an old couple came to the palace kitchen, selling firewood. After the sale was complete, the two sat under that very tree to rest before their journey home. As they sat, a large quince fell into the old woman's lap.

"What a good thing this great fruit did not land on your head, Wife," the husband said, and they both laughed. The wife put the fruit in her apron pocket, saying it would make a good meal that evening. But when they got home, she decided it was not yet quite ripe, so she placed the fruit in an earthen jar to eat another day.

The next morning the couple went out as usual to gather firewood to sell. When they returned, the house was clean and tidy, and a meal of steaming rice sat ready for their dinner. The old couple searched everywhere but could find no trace of the kind stranger who had done these favors.

The next day the very same thing happened, and again the couple could not solve the mystery. So on the third morning the old woman got up extra early and in a loud voice called to her husband. "Get up, lazy bones. We must get an early start to reach the far side of the forest this morning."

"Ha," called the husband. "It is you who are the lazy bones. I am ready and just waiting for you." Together they went out, slamming the door behind them. They walked only a short distance before they crept back and slipped quietly into the cottage to see what would happen.

Just as the sun rose, a tiny woman climbed out of the clay jar and ran into the kitchen. "It is a fruit maiden," whispered the delighted wife, "and I know how to catch her." So saying she fetched one of her best *longyis*. Spreading it near the clay jar, she gave a short yelp. Of course, the frightened maiden ran quickly back toward the jar, whereupon the old wife threw the skirt, capturing her.

When the old woman peered at her tiny captive, she gasped in astonishment, for she immediately recognized who it was. "*A-ma-le!* You are our Queen!" she cried, "We must take you to the King immediately!"

At first, Ma Chit Su begged the old couple not to take her to the palace, for she was afraid the King would punish Ma Ga Hsoh if he knew what had happened. She still did not wish her any harm. But, she missed her husband immensely and longed to be with him again, so finally she agreed.

When the old couple arrived at the palace, they were at once taken to the King. With great joy, he watched Ma Chit Su step from the old woman's basket and bow to him. Promptly, he summoned the false Queen.

"Who are you?" he demanded once again.

The false Queen grew pale as she stared at the fruit maiden, but again protested, "I am your true wife, Ma Chit Su." This wicked fairy who stands before you has bewitched you all."

But the old couple told the King all they knew. Then Ma Chit Su explained how she had been changed first into an egret and then into a fruit maiden.

Before the angry King could order a punishment, Ma Ga Hsoh shouted, "I demand trial by ordeal!"

Now, in such a trial, the contestants must fight with swords. The accuser is given a sword of iron, while the defendant has only a sword made of wood. It is believed that if the defendant has spoken truly, even a wooden sword would defeat an iron one. But Ma Ga Hsoh did not believe these old myths. She felt certain her iron sword would easily defeat Ma Chit Su's wooden one.

Ma Ga Hsoh grinned with malice as she stood facing the tiny fruit maiden, but as she lifted her iron sword, the fruit maiden chanted, "If I am truly Ma Chit Su, let my stepsister's sword become harmless to me." Then she stood there calmly, not wielding her sword at all.

The furious Ma Ga Hsoh flailed and whacked, but whenever the iron sword touched the true Queen, the stroke became as soft as velvet, and with each touch, Ma Chit Su began to grow until at last she had regained her full stature.

In fright, Ma Ga Hsoh threw down her iron sword, realizing at last that some benevolent spirit must indeed guard Ma Chit Su. The gentle-hearted Queen turned to her husband and was about to beg him to pardon Ma Ga Hsoh when, suddenly, the wooden sword jumped from her hands, and, of its own accord, cut off the stepsister's head.

The King, well pleased at this, decided the stepmother must be punished as well. He did not tell his gentle wife, for she would never have consented. Nevertheless, he ordered the false Queen to be cut into small pieces, pickled, and placed in a jar. The jar was then to be delivered to the stepmother with a message saying this was a special gift of pickled fish, prepared by the Queen herself.

Oh how Daw Hla Doke bowed and laughed when the servants arrived at her cottage with the gift. She ran from neighbor to neighbor, boasting how her daughter, the Queen herself, had sent this fine large jar of pickled fish. But the neighbors, disgusted by the boastful woman, wanted no part of it, nor did the old fisherman who had long since tired of his wife's chatter and constant bragging.

That night, with their evening rice, Daw Hla Doke served herself a generous portion of the "pickled fish" as she continued to chatter and gloat.

"Be quiet, old woman, and eat your pickle!" grumbled the husband.

For several days it was the same. Then, one night, Daw Hla Doke pulled out a piece of pickle.

"*A-ma-le!*" she shouted. "This looks like a finger. My daughter's finger."

"Rubbish!" the husband growled. "Eat your pickle and be silent, old woman!"

Discarding the strange bit of pickle, the stepmother drew out another.

"*A-ma-le!*" she cried again. "This looks like a toe. My daughter's toe!"

"You are mad, old woman!" the fisherman shouted, "Be silent, I say!"

Again she discarded the troubling piece. Then Daw Hla Doke looked into the bottom of the clay jar to see whether any pickle remained. To her horror, she thought she saw a face floating in the brine, the pock-marked face of her daughter.

At this point, the disgusted old fisherman beats his wife and the story ends. In Buddhist thought there is no need for "comeuppance" in this world, as the offender will be repaid by a lowly or miserable rebirth in his next life. But we Westerners like to see some justice done in the here and now, so the following has been added.

The evil woman fell screaming to the ground, flailing her arms insanely and ranting about her lovely daughter, her beautiful daughter, her daughter the Queen. Soon she lay dead on the cottage floor.

All this was too much for the old fisherman who walked to his sampan and rowed out to sea where a Naga Dragon rose up from the waves, swallowing him in one gulp.

The Snake Prince

In Burma, all snakes are respected, and many are dangerous, so not surprisingly, the mythical Naga is a frequent figure in Burmese folk tales. In this story, which echoes some aspects of "Beauty and the Beast," Naga resembles an ordinary python and behaves much as a human might. More often, the Naga is shown as a huge Dragon-snake, a sort of Burmese Pluto or Neptune, who rules beneath the earth or under the sea. His origin seems to be the nine-headed snake of Hindu mythology, Lord of Fertility and Death. Many Burmese still hold a superstitious regard for the Naga, and, until very recently, some non-Buddhist hill tribe cults still worshiped the Great Dragon.

There was once an old widow whose cottage stood on the bank of a river not far from the sea. She supported her three daughters by gathering firewood to sell. And each day, while she was in the forest, she would glean any fruit that had fallen from the forest trees. There was one tree in particular, a fine old fig tree, to which the old woman went daily. Its figs were sweet and nourishing.

One morning when she went into the forest, she found not a single fig lying on the ground beneath the fig tree. Angrily, the old widow cried aloud, "Who has stolen my figs? Only a low down dacoit would treat a poor old widow so badly!"

In reply, she heard an angry hiss. Looking up, she saw a huge snake, a python, draped along the branches, glaring at her. In his coils were dozens of ripe figs.

"Oh, Lord Naga, forgive my words," the frightened woman cried. But the Python simply glared.

"Lord Naga," she pleaded. "I have three beautiful daughters. They will be hungry if I can bring them no figs. Perhaps you would like to wed one of them in exchange for some figs?"

The huge snake tilted his head as if to listen to the old woman. Feeling encouraged, she called out again, "Lord Naga, if you would like to wed Ma U, my eldest daughter, please throw down a fig. Even one fig would do." To her surprise, the snake unwound one coil, and threw down one fig.

Encouraged, she called again, "Lord Naga, If you would like to wed Ma Lat, my middle daughter, please drop a fig." The snake unwound a second coil and threw down a second fig.

Feeling quite bold by now, the old widow called once more. "Lord Naga, my youngest daughter, Ma Htwe, is both kind and beautiful. If you would like her for a bride, please throw down a third fig."

At this the snake uncoiled completely, dropping dozens of figs on the ground. Then he shook the branches, causing still more dozens to fall. The delighted widow gathered them up until her basket was overflowing. "Thank you, Lord Naga," she shouted over her shoulder as she hurried down the path towards her cottage.

Along the way she passed a Tree Stump. "Greetings, Old Woman," called the Tree Stump. "What a fine harvest of figs you have in your basket."

"Yes, yes. Indeed I have," answered the woman. "And I will give you one if you will tell the snake, who might be following me, that I did not come this way."

The Tree Stump agreed, so the old woman gave him a fig and hurried on. Soon she passed a Hillock. "Greetings, Old Woman," called the Hillock. "What a fine harvest of figs you have in your basket."

"Yes, yes. Indeed I have," she answered again. "And I will give you one if you will just tell the snake, who might be following me, that I did not come this way."

The Hillock agreed, so the old woman gave him a fig, and hurried on.

Next she passed a Boulder. "Greetings, Old Woman," called the Boulder. "What a fine harvest of figs you have in your basket."

"Yes, yes. Indeed I have," she answered again. "And I will give you one if you will just tell the snake who might be following me, that I did not come this way."

The Boulder agreed, so the old woman gave him a fig also and hurried away.

In a short while she reached her own cottage, and believing she had outwitted the snake, she sat down and laughed heartily.

The Naga, however, was no mere snake. He had seen the old woman before and noticed her three beautiful daughters. He already knew the way to her cottage. Nevertheless, when he passed the Tree Stump he called out, "Greetings, Sir Tree Stump. Did an old woman pass by here this morning?"

The Tree Stump replied, "No, Lord Naga. I have seen no one today."

"Ha," retorted the Naga. "Then how did you get that ripe fig? You are a liar." The frightened Tree Stump stammered an apology and pointed down the path.

Soon, he came to the Hillock. "Greetings, Sir Hillock," he called. "Did an old woman pass by this morning?"

The Hillock replied, "No, Lord Naga. I have seen no one today."

"Ha," retorted the Naga. "Then how did you get that ripe

fig? You are a liar." The frightened Hillock stammered an apology and pointed down the path.

Finally, he came to the Boulder. "Greetings, Sir Boulder," he said. "Did an old woman pass by this morning?"

The Boulder replied, "No, Lord Naga. I have seen no one today."

"Ha," retorted the Naga, "then how did you get that ripe fig? You are a liar." The frightened Boulder stammered an apology and he, too, pointed down the path.

The Naga soon reached the old widow's cottage, climbed the bamboo stilts, and slid into the kitchen. There he curled up in the large earthen jar where the old woman kept her rice.

When it was time to cook the noon meal, the old woman went into the kitchen and opened the jar to take out a measure of rice. The snake immediately coiled himself around her arm, and glared at her. "Woman, you have tried to deceive me," he hissed.

The frightened woman tried to pretend innocence. "Lord Naga," she pleaded. "at the fig tree you appeared to wish to wed one of my daughters. I simply hurried home to prepare them to receive you."

The Naga simply continued to glare at the woman, not mentioning his conversations with the Tree Stump, the Hillock and the Boulder. The woman spoke again. "Lord Naga, if it would please you to wed my eldest daughter, Ma U, please undo one coil." To her relief, the snake unwound one coil.

"Lord Naga," she said feeling somewhat braver, "If it would please you to wed my middle daughter, Ma Lat, please undo a coil." Promptly the snake released a second coil.

Feeling greatly cheered, the old woman said firmly, "Lord

Naga, if it would please you to wed my youngest daughter, Ma Htwe, please unwind a third coil.

At once the snake unwound completely.

By now the woman realized that the snake was determined to marry one of her daughters and would harm her if she did not keep her promise. Privately, she called the three young women to her and told them what had happened that morning.

"Ma U, will you marry the Naga for my sake?" she asked her eldest daughter.

Ma U raised her brow in contempt. "Marry a snake? Certainly not. Surely you do not take his threats seriously!"

The old woman turned to her middle daughter. "Ma Lat, will you marry the Naga for my sake?" she asked.

But Ma Lat wrinkled her nose in horror. "Marry a snake? Certainly not. Surely we can think of some trick to rid ourselves of such a disgusting creature."

Last, the old woman turned to her youngest daughter. "Ma Htwe, will you marry the Naga for my sake?" she asked. By now she was shaking with fear. Ma Htwe took her mother's face in her small hands. "Do not be afraid, dearest Mother. I will gladly marry the Naga for your sake. I will be a dutiful and loving wife and tend all his needs."

Ma Htwe went to the Naga with her finest basket lined with soft cotton. "You may rest in here, if it please you, Lord Naga," she said. Then she stroked his smooth brow and brought him milk and rice, and when night came Ma Htwe carried the basket and placed it beside her bed. She lit one candle to the Buddha and one to Thagya Min. Then she said her evening prayers and went to bed.

In the night she had a strange dream. In her dream, a tall

young Prince came to her bed and held her tenderly. She had the same dream the next night and again a third night. As it puzzled her, she spoke of it to her mother.

"It is probably a good omen," said the mother. "I will go ask the astrologer what he makes of such a dream." But the old woman did not ask the astrologer. Instead, the next night, after her daughters were asleep, the old woman crept from her bed and slipped into Ma Htwe's room, hiding behind a chest in the corner.

When midnight arrived, the woman heard a rustling sound and she saw a handsome youth step from the basket. She watched him walk to Ma Htwe's bed, slip in beside her, and embrace her tenderly.

The old woman waited until she was certain they were both asleep, then she crept back into the kitchen, taking the basket with her. Just as she had expected, there, in the bottom of the basket, lay a snake skin. She promptly snatched it up and threw it into the fire.

With a cry of great pain, the Prince came running into the kitchen.

"Old Mother," he pleaded, "give me my skin. Mercy on me, for I burn and will surely die."

The shouts of pain awoke Ma Htwe who came running into the kitchen. There she saw the Prince writhing on the floor, his skin red and blistering. Immediately, she poured cool water over him, then she soothed his burns with oil of palm and camphor, sweetened with jasmine. When the Prince's pain had eased, he sat up and took Ma Htwe's hand. "As your mother has guessed," he said, "I am a Naga Prince. But, as she has burned my skin I must remain in this form, a mortal like you. Like you, I will now grow old as the years pass, and one day, like you, I will die. But with you at my side, dear, kind Ma Htwe, I know my years will be happy."

Part Two: The Wicked Sisters

Ma Htwe's sisters clearly envied her good fortune. They were spiteful and quarreled with her constantly, so after a short time, Ma Htwe and the Snake Prince built a cottage of their own on a high bank near the sea. They planted a garden of roses and jasmine and cabbages and sweet-smelling herbs. In the evening they would sit together in their hammock, rocking gently as the orange sun dropped beyond the distant hills.

Their joy seemed complete when, after a time, a son was born to them. They named him Kin Shwe, Prince Golden, and spoiled him with love and many toys, which his father carved for him. Each day, the Prince gathered reeds from the riverbank and Ma Htwe wove them into baskets to sell in the bazaar. These brought coins enough for rice and the other things they needed, but not enough for silk scarves or silver chains or ruby broaches.

"I must find a better trade," the Snake Prince said one day. "What kind of Prince cannot provide fine things for his wife and son?"

Ma Htwe just laughed. "You are all the treasure we need," she told him.

One day, a merchant ship from a distant land sailed up the river, stopping at their village. It carried silks and spices, exquisitely worked leather, and ornaments suitable for a king's palace. Now, at last, the Prince knew what he would do.

"Beloved," he told Ma Htwe, "I shall become a merchant

and sail across the seas. I will miss you terribly, but until I can give you the fine things a Prince's wife should have, I shall never be truly content." Then the Snake Prince gathered many bushels of rice and baskets of dried fish. He cut many cords of firewood and built a great clay cistern, which he filled with water. All these he stored within the inner walls of the cottage garden. When he had finished, he took his wife's hands in his and made her promise that she would not leave the safety of their cottage, for he feared that the jealous sisters might harm Ma Htwe or their son. Then, kissing Kin Shwe on the forehead, he sailed away.

As soon as Ma U and Ma Lat learned that the Prince had left, they plotted ways to kill Ma Htwe, just out of spite. Besides, each thought secretly, the Snake Prince might choose to marry her when he returned.

One morning, they went their sister's cottage and called. "Dearest sister. We are going to the bazaar to buy rice. Come with us. We miss your company."

But Ma Htwe answered that she had enough rice and that she was busy playing cat's cradle with her tiny son, Kin Shwe. A second day they went to her cottage and called, "Dearest sister. We are going to the forest to gather firewood. Do come with us. We miss your company." Again Ma Htwe answered that she had all the wood she needed and that she busy washing Kin Shwe's hair.

On a third day, the wicked sisters went to Ma Htwe's cottage and called to her, "Dearest sister. We are going to the spring to draw fresh water. If you come with us, we can help you carry back the heavy jars." Once again, Ma Htwe answered that her cistern held all the water she needed, and besides she was busy weaving a new wicker ball, a *chinlon*, for Kin Shwe.

For the next three days Ma Htwe heard nothing from her wicked sisters. Then, one bright morning she heard them running past her cottage, laughing and singing as they went. Curious, she peered out a window. Her sisters carried a picnic basket, and they were chasing butterflies across the grasses.

"Hello, sisters," Ma Htwe called. "You seem so merry. Is there some festival I have forgotten?"

"No, no." The sisters answered. "We are just taking a picnic to the old mango tree. It has been many months since we have been there to play on the swing."

Ma Htwe sighed, remembering the sturdy old tree and the many happy times she and her sisters had spent swinging together there by the edge of the sea.

"I wish I could come," she said half aloud.

"Ha," Ma Lat called back. "We don't want you. Every time we ask you to come with us, you are too busy with this or that."

"You have become too proud," called Ma U. "Stay inside with your precious princeling. You are no longer any fun." And the sisters joined hands and ran on across the meadow.

"How can they be plotting against me?" Ma Htwe thought aloud. "They don't even want me to come." So, picking up Tin Shwe, Ma Htwe ran out of the cottage and down the path after her sisters.

When they reached the mango tree, the cross words were forgotten. The three sisters laughed and ate yellow rice together and played happily with little Tin Shwe.

"Remember how we always took turns?" cried Ma U, running to sit on the swing. The other two laughed and helped start the swing rocking.

"Now it is my turn," called Ma Lat after a time. Ma U slowed the swing and got off. Then she and Ma Htwe rocked the swing for Ma Lat. At last it was Ma Htwe's turn. Innocently, she climbed on, holding Tin Shwe close to her. "This is great fun," she told her small son who just pulled at her hair, gurgling happily.

Ma U and Ma Lat got behind the swing to push, but they gave it such a shove that Ma Htwe sailed high into the air, lost her balance, and fell into the sea. The wicked sisters ran to the edge of the bluff to watch the waves carry Ma Htwe and her son out to sea, then they ran home gleefully, satisfied that Ma Htwe would never trouble them again.

By great good fortune, a large stork flew by, hunting for fish. He saw Ma Htwe struggling in the water and promptly snatched her from the water, carrying her and the child to his nest high in a tree on an island many miles from the shore.

The old bird gazed at his prize with satisfaction. "What a pretty wife you are," he told Ma Htwe, "and now I have a fine son as well!" Then he flew away to catch fish for her supper.

When he returned, Ma Htwe tried to explain to the stork that she already had a husband, and that neither she nor her son cared for raw fish, but the silly old stork wouldn't listen.

That night she rocked her son to sleep, singing: "Hush, my baby, Son of the Snake Prince."

The angry stork shouted that he would peck her with his big beak if she kept singing such nonsense. So she sang again: "Hush, my baby, Son of the Stork Bird."

This so pleased the stork that he laughed loudly and settled down to sleep. Night after night, the same thing happened, for Ma Htwe constantly thought of her beloved. She never stopped hoping that one day she might see him again, and it gave her comfort to sing out his name.

After some months, the Prince's merchant ship passed near

the island on its return voyage. The ship approached at dusk, and the sailors heard the strange song of the woman and the raucous laughter of the stork. They thought sea spirits were about to do them some evil, so they ran to the Snake Prince, begging him to listen.

The Prince at once knew the voice to be that of his beloved and commanded the sailors to drop anchor. Then the Prince rowed to the shore. The stork, seeing the Prince from his treetop, flew at him, ready to attack. But just as the Prince drew his sword, Ma Htwe shouted at them both.

"Please don't fight, but first hear my story." And Ma Htwe told the Prince all that had happened, explaining how the stork had saved her and her child from the sea.

The Prince bowed. "I thank you, good Stork, and now I will take my wife and child home with me.

"No, no!" shouted the stork. "I rescued them. They are mine!" And again he poised his beak as if to fight.

"Don't be such a foolish old bird," replied the Prince. "Can't you see I could easily kill you with my sword? Further, I have five hundred sailors to call to my assistance."

Back and forth the two argued, the stubborn stork wanting to fight a duel, and the Prince trying to find some way to win his family without killing the stork. At last, the Prince said, "Sir Stork, which would you rather have, my wife and child, or five hundred fish?"

The stork suddenly felt hungry after so much arguing. "Why, five hundred fish, of course," he answered.

At this the Prince ordered his sailors to cast nets, and in a short time piled them on the island under the stork's tree. For his part of the bargain, the stork carried Ma Htwe and her son safely to the Prince's ship. The Prince embraced them warmly and gave the order to sail on.

"Those treacherous sisters of yours must die," the Prince muttered angrily. But Ma Htwe pleaded with him to spare their lives. Seeing how much this meant to her, he agreed. "But at the least they must be shamed." he said, and the two discussed a plan.

The Prince emptied a heavy chest, lined it with silk and pillows and bored some breathing holes in its side. Then, Ma Htwe and their son climbed in. As the ship approached their village, Ma Lat and Ma U hurried to dress in their best clothes and set jasmine into their hair. Then they hurried down to greet the Prince. Indeed the whole village waited at the dock.

"Where is my Ma Htwe?" the Prince demanded of the sisters as he stepped off the ship.

"Oh, Lord Naga," Ma Lat cried out. "She fell into the sea one day and no one could rescue her for the stormy waves beating on the rocks."

"We are very sad to bring you such news," said Ma U. "But allow us to comfort you. My sister and I have agreed. You may choose one of us, or even both of us, for a new wife."

The Prince looked at them sadly. "You are most kind, but I could not marry again so soon," he said. Then he sat down and mopped his brow.

"Your news has weakened me," he continued. "Unfortunately, I shall now have to ask my sailors to carry the chest that rests in my cabin. I had intended to carry it myself for fear my sailors might run off with it. Its treasure exceeds that of all my other chests combined."

"We will carry it for you," exclaimed the sisters. They had been watching greedily as the sailors carried bales of silk and many ironbound chests to the Prince's cottage.

"Oh, that is most thoughtful!" said the Prince. "It was for Ma Htwe, but as you tell me she is now dead, you may as well carry the chest to your own cottage. As my wife's nearest kin, I suppose, the treasure should now be yours.

Eagerly, the two sisters ran to the ship and found the large chest in the Prince's cabin. It was extremely heavy, but the two sisters tugged and pulled and heaved. They would not accept any help for fear they might have to share the gold and jewels the chest surely contained.

After much sweating and effort they reached their cottage. The neighbors stood about, eager to see what was in so valuable a chest. Boastfully, the sisters turned the key the Prince had given them, unclasped the lock and opened the chest.

To their horror, out stepped Ma Htwe and her son. The neighbors roared with laughter at the joke and jeered at the sisters who ran with shame into their cottage. Although Ma Htwe forgave them, the two sisters never again had honor among the people of the village and for gentle Ma Htwe, that was punishment enough.

There is a second ending in which the greedy sisters, jealous of Ma Htwe's luck, demand that their mother find them a Snake Prince also. After weeks of hunting, the mother brings home a large and sleepy python and places it beside her middle daughter's bed. Of course, being just an ordinary snake, it wakes and swallows the sister, after which the eldest daughter leaves well enough alone.

The Tiny Flute Player

If you draw a face on your thumbnail and small feet on your knuckle, you will see what a very tiny person this story is about. Almost every country has such a story, telling of a tiny child who has wonderful adventures.

On the very day Ah Sein was born, he fell through a narrow split in the floor matting, for he was no larger than a *toc-toc* (a small lizard). His frantic mother raced around the house looking under baskets and jars, calling, "Where are you, my son, my precious diamond?"

By climbing up one of the house posts, the child soon scrambled back into the room. In his hand he clutched a tiny flute made from a splinter of bamboo.

"Here I am, Mother," he called, popping up through the hole. "See what I have made?" And at once he sat on the mat and began a merry tune.

Old Daw Yiu laughed happily at this wonderful son of hers. Plucking him up, she held him gently in her cupped hands, swaying and dancing to his music. Not for nothing had she named him Ah Sein, for had he not been born on Sunday under the protection of the great Galon bird? And was he not as precious to her as any diamond?

"Mother," Ah Sein announced as soon as the tune was finished, "all this playing has left me very hungry. Please cook me some rice."

Daw Yiu cooked a large quantity, enough to fill her best and largest red lacquered *huaminok*, thinking that would feed them all. But to her astonishment, the tiny boy ate every grain, and she had to cook a second basket for herself and her husband.

For many weeks, Ah Sein did nothing but play his flute and eat great quantities of rice. Daily, the annoyed father, who was a poor rice farmer, exclaimed, "Ah Sein, indeed. He should be called Pho Shoke, for he is a bother and a nuisance, and is good for nothing whatsoever!"

After more weeks, the old farmer looked into his rice jars to see how much remained. How rapidly they seemed to empty! "Old woman," he said to his wife, "your gluttonous son will be our death! Tomorrow I will take him into the forest when I go to gather wood. There, I will kill and bury him where no one will know. Then there will be rice enough for us, and besides, I will no longer have to listen to his incessant fluting."

Daw Yiu's eyes widened in horror. She clasped her hands in supplication, and wept. "No, no, no!" she cried. "Not my precious one, my Sunday's child, my diamond!" The old farmer frowned, but he heeded her wish and did no harm to the child.

Week after week, as more rice jars grew empty, the husband repeated his threat, and week after week, he yielded to Daw Yiu's frantic pleas. At last, only one full rice jar remained. This time the old man insisted, and sorrowfully, Daw Yiu consented.

"Promise just one thing," she pleaded. "Do not kill him by your own hand, but arrange some accident. And if, after four attempts, he remains alive—you must never again plot to harm him."

The old husband promised, certain that one accident would do nicely.

The next day he asked his son to come with him into the forest. They walked until they reached an especially large tree. "Stand there, Pho Shoke," the father commanded. "This tree will provide much wood for your mother."

The obedient boy stood where his father had pointed, playing a merry tune while the old man chopped. Of course, the tree fell on the very spot where the tiny flute-player stood, and the pleased father hurried home.

"At last I am rid of this bothersome son," thought the old man. But just as he started up the steps to his house, Ah Sein came down the path, carrying the tree on his back.

"Hello, Father," he shouted. "This tree fell on my back. I caught it and have brought it home for you. Shall I put it near the wood pile?" The dismayed old husband nodded. The tiny boy put down the tree and began again to play his flute.

The first try had failed. The old farmer stopped his ears with cotton and tried to think of another plan.

The next day, he asked Ah Sein to come with him, saying he had business with the Sayadaw at the *kyaung* a few miles away. Together, they walked along the high road, the child fluting merrily as they went.

As the father expected, a herd of elephants soon came down the road. While they were still a long way off, the father said, "Wait there, Pho Shoke. I will be back shortly." The old man pointed to a spot in the very middle of the road, then hurried into the bushes to tend his need, or so Ah Sein assumed.

Playing first one tune and then another, the boy waited obediently. The *oozies* (elephant drivers), hearing the merry tune, looked up and down the road to see who the musician might be, but could see no one.

"Make way, make way," they shouted, driving their elephants forward. Just as the lead elephant's great foot hovered above him, Ah Sein jumped into the hoofprint of a cow, and remained there safely as the herd trod overhead.

When the elephants were out of sight, the old farmer started back to the road, but to his dismay, the sound of the boy's flute filled the air once more.

Frowning, he lifted his son with two fingers and tucked him into his Shan bag, saying, "We must return home after all, for I have forgotten one of the letters I meant to ask the Sayadaw to read to me."

Now, twice he had tried to rid himself of this gluttonous son who daily ate as much rice as a full grown man. That night, the father lay awake scheming.

The next morning, he asked Ah Sein to go with him to the river to fish. When the boat was far from shore, the father tipped the boat as if by accident, and flailing with the oar, knocked the lad into the swift current.

Thinking that this time he was surely rid of his bothersome child, the old man rowed back, smiling to himself. But before he reached the shore, the merry sound of a flute again filled the air. There, at the water's edge, sat the tiny boy, astride the neck of a large crocodile.

"Hello, Father," Ah Sein called cheerfully. "See this fine water lizard I have caught for you?"

"No, no, Son. Thank you, but we do not want such a lizard," the father called out. So the boy jumped into his father's boat, and the bewildered crocodile swam away. For a third time, the father's plans had failed.

That night, Daw Yiu cooked the last of the rice. She sighed as they shared their meager meal, but Ah Sein just played another fine tune and set his mother dancing in spite of herself.

On the fourth morning, the father again took Ah Sein into the forest. "We must gather breadfruit and papaya until the new rice is ready for thrashing," he told the boy.

This time they traveled on and on, high into the mountains. All through the journey, the child continued to play on his flute. Birds called back, and monkeys scampered along the branches, dancing to the merry music. As usual, the father had stuffed still more cotton into his ears and wound a strip of cloth over them as well.

By noon they reached a great banyon in the thickest, wildest part of the jungle. There they sat to eat the boiled greens and bananas Daw Yiu had prepared for them. When they had finished, the old father stretched out on the ground for a nap while the child ran about, chasing small lizards and playing his flute.

The minute Ah Sein ran out of sight, the old man jumped up and hurried home along a different path. "At last, I am rid of that noisy boy," he told himself, certain the child could never find his way back alone.

The boy, running back into the small clearing, discovered his father gone. "Oh, my poor father. He must be looking for me," Ah Sein thought and he began calling, "Here I am, Father. Here I am." For a while he searched and called. At last, he started for home, hoping his father might have done the same.

On his way he passed the den of a tiger who woke at the smell of flesh. The tiger lifted his great head and began to creep toward his prey.

Just as he was about to pounce, Ah Sein put his flute to his lips and began to play. The tiger froze, terrified that such a tiny being could make so loud a sound. "This must be a fearsome Nat in disguise," the tiger thought. Humbly, he allowed the tiny flute-player to jump on his neck and ride him through the jungle and down the mountain.

When Ah Sein reached home on his unusual steed, he was

delighted to see his father, safely home and talking with a neighbor.

"Hello, Father," Ah Sein shouted. "You need not worry any longer. I am home safely, too. And see what a fine big kitty I have brought you!" The boy jumped off the tiger, and the terrified animal turned and streaked back into the forest.

Daw Yiu ran down the house ladder and joyfully scooped Ah Sein into her arms. "Oh, my Precious, my Sunday's child, my Diamond! You are safe."

And indeed he was, for by now even the father had to admit that the tiny flute player was a pretty wonderful little fellow after all.

Pulling the cotton from his ears, the old man joined his wife in a merry dance while the tiny boy played tune after tune after tune.

The Burmese story ends here, but perhaps, Ah Sein used his skill with animals to help harvest the rice and plant for the coming year. And perhaps the neighbor had come with some rice to tide the family over the next few weeks. That would not be unlike the Burmese. Each morning, most Buddhist households give rice to the pongyis, *partly for "merit" and partly because a thoughtful concern for others is natural among them.*

The Three Dragon Eggs

In some folk tales from the dry hot central plains of Burma, the sun is cast as a villain. But in this story from the northern hills, the sun is a handsome Prince, able to scorch a crow's feathers in anger, but missed by the villagers when he lingers too long by a mountain lake. Here, the Naga princess is a silver-scaled dragon whose home is at the bottom of a lake.

In the high, cool mountains of Northern Burma, a beautiful Naga once lived at the bottom of an ice blue lake. Sometimes a fisherman would see her silver body slip through the waves. He would rush back to the village to share the news. Then everyone would run to the shore, hoping for a glimpse. But of course, by then, the Naga would have hidden in the deep.

This particular Naga was a young Princess, full of curiosity and wonder. Often she watched laughing groups of village girls come to bathe and wash their shining black hair. Mothers with babes came to fill jars with the clear lake water for their homes. Shepherd lads brought their goats to drink on their way to the high alp pastures, and occasionally, strong young hunters came to rest beside the quiet lake.

One day, longing to see more, and feeling bold, the Naga Princess took human form, emerged from the lake, and climbed to a high rock, where she sat warming herself in the bright sunlight. The Sun, passing overhead, saw the young woman and was instantly dazzled by her great beauty.

The next day, and the next, the Princess came and sat on the rock, and each day the Sun longed more and more to be with her. At last he could bear it no longer. Early one morning, when he should have started his journey across the blue arch of heaven, the Sun took the form of a hunter and came through the forest blowing a haunting tune on his bamboo flute.

The Naga Princess looked about for the source of the beautiful sound and saw a young man approaching. As she turned to run, the youth smiled and begged her to stay. His smile pleased her greatly and she lingered.

For many days they met morning and evening. Their love grew strong and they vowed to cherish each other forever. But soon, the people of the village started to grumble and complain, asking why the Sun arrived so late and departed so early, why the days were no longer warmed by his rays, and the millet would not grow. "Come back to us, Oh Sun," they cried.

The Sun could see their distress. "Beloved," he said sadly, "I must go back to my duties, but I shall leave my white crow with you, and when our children are born, send him to me with the glad news. They shall be well cared for. And in the month of Nadaw, I will come again and bide with you awhile." The Princess kissed him tearfully and bade him farewell.

Some months later, when the days and weeks were fulfilled, the Naga Princess gave birth to three splendid eggs. At once she sent the crow to tell her husband the good news.

The Sun welcomed the crow. "Wait," he said. "I have a gift for her." He went to his treasure store and brought out an enormous ruby of great worth. "Take this to my beloved," he told the crow. "Tell her of my great joy—and of my regret that I cannot come at once to see the children. Instruct her to purchase a kingdom with this jewel so that one day my children can rule over it." Then, wrapping the ruby in fine gauze, he placed it in a white silk pouch, embroidered with gold threads and closed with gold cords. Then he charged the crow to carry it back to his beloved.

As the crow flew above the forest, he spied a caravan of merchants. They were cooking rice and delicious-smelling curries and laughing and telling jokes. Hungry and eager to enjoy their company, the white crow flew to the branch of a jack-fruit tree. Tucking his treasure in a notch, he settled in their midst, gulping the morsels they tossed and cawing raucously to join their laughter.

One merchant, aware that white crows were often messengers of the spirit kingdom, looked about. Spying the silken packet, he went among the bushes as if to relieve himself. Instead, he circled stealthily back to examine his find.

When the merchant opened the pouch and saw the enormous ruby, he gasped. "What great, great, good fortune has come my way," he thought. Slipping the gem into his own pouch, he filled the silk one with a large clod of dung, and returned to the laughing group unnoticed. Unaware of the treachery, the white crow continued on to the Princess.

The Naga Princess saw the crow returning and welcomed him with food and water. Eagerly, she untied the golden cord and opened the silken pouch, but when she found it filled with dung, her heart broke. Surely such an insult meant her Prince no longer loved her. In despair, the Naga Princess retreated to the deepest shadows of the nether world, never again to emerge into the Sun's light, or to see the water sparkle in his golden rays.

The month of Nadaw arrived, and, just as the Sun had promised, he returned to the mountain lake. Indeed he came year after year, morning and evening, to sit by the water's edge waiting and alone.

For a long while the eggs lay abandoned and with no mother to care for them they could not hatch. However, the mountain spirits took pity on the neglected eggs and working what transformations they could, asked the melting snows to wash the eggs into the rushing streams that flowed down the mountain and thence into the great Irrawaddy.

In Northern Burma, at Mogok, the first dragon egg caught in an eddy at the foot of some cliffs and broke open. Out spilled a great flood of rubies, emeralds, and precious stones of every variety to mingle with the clay and sands of the hills. In Middle Burma, the second egg caught on a sandbar. It too, hit a rock and broke open. Out stepped a fierce tiger, whose tribe from that day forward ruled the dark forests of all Jambudipa.

In Lower Burma, where the great river branches into myriad streams, the last egg smashed against the roots of a mangrove. From the egg emerged a great crocodile, whose tribe ever since has ruled the turgid delta waters of all Jambudipa. When at last the Sun learned what had happened, he sought the neglectful crow and scorched his feathers black.

An almost identical tale from Central Burma purports to tell the origin of a semi-historical Pyu King called Sawhti (or Sawdi). In that story, the first egg also spills gems at Mogok, a very real place that has produced some of the world's most prized rubies. The second egg produces a beautiful girl child who later becomes Queen of an unnamed country, while the third egg holds the future Prince Sawhti, who is then brought up by a hermit.

This youth later rids Pagan of four terrible monsters, using the magical sword, lance, and demon horse that the spirit King, Thagya Min, had once given his father. No reference is made to the celestial orb being absent from the sky. Indeed, near the equator, the time of year makes very little difference in the length of daylight, and the seasons are three: the hot season, the cool season, and the wet season.

The Tickling Nat

Nats are found less often in Burmese folk tales than in the everyday lives and behavior of the people. In its original version, this tale has the qualities of a fable. Names are omitted. The son shows no remorse, the young wife no temper. She only complains that the old woman eats too much rice.

Ma Khin was not well named, for her name meant Miss Lovable. There was no doubt Ma Khin was pretty, possibly the prettiest young woman in the village. All the young men courted her, but it was Maung At Ni she wed.

The old *Pônna* astrologer advised against it. So did the marriage broker. But At Ni was adamant. Since the widow, Daw Thet, usually let her son have his way, he prevailed in this as well. And now the three lived together in old Daw Thet's bamboo house.

This did not please Ma Khin, for she wished to run the house. It did not please the mother, as she expected to continue to cook and wash as before. And it did not please At Ni, for his wife was constantly complaining.

"Your mother does not like me," Ma Khin whined. "Each day she trots off to the pagoda with mangoes or sticky rice for the Pongyis and the *nat* shrine. This morning she struck me with the sweeping broom and slopped water on my best *longyi*. Yesterday I even saw her opening my red lacquer jewel box!

"She is old and useless. And see how she eats! Rice! Too much rice!"

The only true thing in all this complaining was that the older woman did not like the younger one, and that Daw Thet did indeed go three times each day to both the Pagoda and the Nat shrine, taking small gifts of food and fresh water and sweet-smelling jasmine.

No! It was Ma Khin who spent much of her day strolling in the market, fingering the fine silks and silver chains. It was Ma Khin who rifled through her mother-in-law's jewel box, touching rings and broaches with covetous thoughts. And it was Ma Khin who had clumsily bumped into Daw Khin that morning, causing the broom to thwack the older woman and water to slop over both their skirts. Indeed, Ma Khin seldom helped at all.

Every evening, when At Ni returned from the forest with his barrow load of wood, Ma Khin whined and complained. The old widow held her tongue, but with each passing week she became more stony-faced and silent. Poor At Ni. How could he please both his mother and his wife? His life had become a misery.

"We should have a fine teak house like Wun Sein, the magistrate," Ma Khin demanded over and over. "How can you abide this miserable bamboo hut, or that wrinkled old woman?"

At Ni would only sigh and shake his head. "The wood I sell barely brings enough for our daily rice. And that old wrinkled woman is my mother who has loved and cared for me all these years!"

"Well she is useless and ugly now!" Ma Khin would retort. "And see how much rice she eats while we skimp and have too little for ourselves." Then she would throw cups and ladles across the room while At Ni covered his ears and pretended to sleep.

Night after night, Ma Khin quarreled and complained, demanding that At Ni get rid of his mother. Before three moons had passed, she began saying, "Take that useless old woman into the forest. Lose her there before we ourselves starve."

"I cannot!" At Ni would cry in alarm. "Besides my mother knows the forest well. She gathered wood along with my father when she was young and strong."

Ma Khin's retort cut like a hunter's dah. "Then bind her to a tree. Let the tigers do what you are too weak to do yourself!"

Before eight moons had passed, At Ni was a mere frazzle, and Ma Khin no longer allowed At Ni into her bed. "Not until your mother is gone!" she would say. At last the day came when At Ni agreed to his wife's demands. That night, she had stalked off to her own bed in another fit of temper. At Ni sat outside on the narrow verandah watching the stars and waiting for his mother to return from her evening devotions at the pagoda.

"Come with me to the forest tomorrow," he pleaded. "We shall have a picnic just like the days when I was small. Remember how you and Father and I shared our noon rice together? Then we would listen to the calling birds and pluck orchids for the *nat* shrine!"

Daw Thet smiled. It had been a long time since she had smiled. "Yes my son. That would indeed be pleasant." Early the next morning, Daw Thet cooked a special sweet rice and wrapped it in a palm leaf packet for their noon meal, and the two set off before the sun's rays glinted on the pagoda spire. All morning At Ni cut firewood while his mother gathered kindling. At noon, Daw Thet boiled water for tea. Then mother and son sat beneath a great tamarind tree, sharing sweet rice and listening to the birds.

"There are tears in your eyes, my son. Why is that?" Daw Thet asked.

"I was remembering Father," At Ni lied as he stirred opium powder into his mother's hot tea. The two then lay back to rest, watching clouds make patterns in the sky while monkeys chattered and tiny creatures rustled the leaves.

Soon Daw Thet fell into a deep sleep. At Ni, tears streaming down his face, bound his unconscious mother to the tree trunk, kissed her forehead, and asked the Buddha and the Nats to keep her asleep while the terrible deed was accomplished.

With a heart heavier than his load of wood, At Ni then lifted the handles of his barrow and set off down the mountain to his cruel wife and ramshackle hut. The Nat of the tamarind tree, watching all this, remembered At Ni as a small loving boy. She wondered what had driven the young man to such cruel behavior.

That night as the first star blinked in the sky, three fine, strong tigers came from the depths of the jungle. Seeing the sleeping woman tied there, they stretched out their claws and murmured a satisfied rumble.

"Hold on there, you fellows," the Nat said, stepping down from the branches. "I want to tickle her and find out what sort of woman she is!"

"Oh, very well," said the strongest tiger, eyeing his prey. The Nat took a white egret feather and brushed it under Daw Thet's nose.

"*A-choo, A-choo,*" she sneezed, and seeing the tigers glaring at her, she cried out, "Buddha, Buddha, be thou my refuge." So saying, she closed her eyes, expecting the tigers to pounce at once.

"Go away, Tigers!" the Nat commanded. "This is a good woman and you must not eat her." Of course Daw Thet could neither see nor hear the spirit. She only knew the tigers did not pounce, and when at last she dared to peek, she saw them walking away, swishing their tails hungrily.

Thanking the Lord Buddha and whatever spirits had protected her, she fell back into her drugged sleep. At dawn Daw Thet awoke refreshed. The ropes had been cut and she lay on the soft moss with large pot of gold beside her.

Making a net of her bonds, the old woman started to drag the pot of gold down the mountain. On her way, she met her son, half blind from weeping, trudging back up the mountain with his empty woodcutter's barrow. Seeing his mother alive, he shouted for joy and fell at her feet, begging her to forgive him.

Daw Thet shook her head, sadly. "I love you, my son, but the spirits of heaven will have to do that," she said. "For I cannot."

At Ni nodded, then gently lifted his mother and the pot of gold onto the barrow and wheeled it back to the village. The magistrate, Wun Sein, gladly sold Daw Thet a fine teak house like his own, and soon she was living a comfortable life.

When Ma Khin discovered her mother-in-law was not only alive, but wealthy as well, the young woman flew into a terrible tantrum. She soon learned the story of Daw Thet's good fortune from gossiping neighbors, for At Ni, refusing to return to her, had taken refuge with the monks.

At once Ma Khin went to the monastery, demanding that her husband take her to the forest and tie her to the tamarind tree. That night, as the first evening star appeared, Ma Khin watched three tigers padding toward her through the forest.

"What good luck, Brothers," said one tiger. "Here is another fine dinner, fatter and younger and more tender than that old woman who was here a few nights ago." And the three stretched their claws and bared their teeth.

Ma Khin smiled, unafraid, for she remembered Daw Thet's good fortune.

Just as before, the Tree Spirit stepped from the branches and told the tigers they must wait until she had a chance to tickle the young woman. The Nat took her white egret feather and brushed it under Ma Khin's nose.

"A-choo, a-choo," she sneezed. "Now, give me my pot of gold!"

The Nat turned to the drooling tigers. "You are welcome to eat this greedy, heartless woman," she said. Which they did at once.

❦

Part II: Crafty Villains, Clever Opponents, and Fools

Pwē: Stories in Dance & Song

The Burmese love to laugh, especially at the clever villain, the dull-witted but lucky drunkard, or some completely illogical ending. It matters little whether the outcome is fair. The villain will get his comeuppance, if only in his next life.

All these paradoxical elements meet in the popular, open-air performances called *pwé*. This is Burmese opera: an eclectic mix of instrumental music, song, dance, clowning, and dramatized stories lasting from early evening to dawn. Often the moon is full and the sky clear and full of stars, for dry season is the time of *pwé*, and every full moon deserves some celebration.

The benefactor will hire a troupe, have a platform or *maidan* built in an open field, and spread out bamboo matting for the guests. The *pwé* is his gift to the community, perhaps to celebrate the birth of a child, a daughter's wedding, a son's *shin-pyu*, a temple festival, or just to earn merit for his next life.

Whole families from all around come with picnic lunches and extra mats. During the performance they will variously chat, sleep, or listen attentively to favorite recitations or songs, the best of which frequently occur well after midnight.

There are favorites, particularly the Indian epic, *The Ramayana,* or the Jatakas. There is always a prince (Min Tha) and a princess (Min Tha Mi), a villain or two, accomplices, and the ubiquitous clowns.

Romantic love is stylized and formal. Not even in drama does etiquette permit touching in public between men and women—except in *yokthe,* or puppet theater. Not being human, the puppets are allowed to embrace. And the clowns are positively bawdy, often shouting suggestive jokes which set the audience roaring with laughter. No one protects the ears of the young or hides the outrageous clowning. This is theater for all, just as folk tales are intended for every age. Knowing the stories and songs and jokes by heart only seems to increase the pleasure.

The Pincers of Pagan

Those magnificent pagodas! Marco Polo saw and wrote about them in his journals. Pagan was a fabulous city, he said, studded with over a thousand pagodas—golden, silver, or gleaming white.

That number was exaggerated, but Pagan was truly a wonder of the ancient world, and Anawrahta Min, who had spurred all that building, spent much of his energy making his kingdom orderly and peaceful. Certainly a mythical object such as these pincers would have been very useful in a kingdom such as his!

In the royal city of Pagan, in the time of the great King Anawrahta, a huge pair of pincers hung in the golden *stupa* of the King's newest pagoda. The King was very proud to have obtained this pair of pincers, for they had the power to distinguish truth from falsehood. The King's judges had only to require the accused party to hold his hands between the pincers and state whether or not he had committed the offense. If the plaintiff lied, the pincers promptly cut off his hands, and if he truly stated that he was guiltless, everyone could be certain that this was so.

Throughout the land, people now kept honestly to their contracts. They refrained from theft or rape or murder, all because of the marvelous pincers. King Anawrahta was very pleased to be King over such harmony and peace. The judges of the land had more time to read from the scriptures or visit with the monks and townspeople. Everyone praised the pincers, and in turn, the pincers rejoiced in the well-deserved honor the people bestowed on them.

There was however, in the nearby monastery, a clever

young novice called Maung Aye Din, who had a covetous nature. He often wondered how a question might be framed in such a way that truth would seem false, and falseness truth.

One day a wealthy merchant from lower Burma came to the monastery, asking that a *viss* of gold be kept safely for him while he traveled to Thailand, beyond the protection and peace of the great kingdom of Pagan. The Sayadaw agreed to keep the *viss* of gold, calling on the young novice to be steward. Maung Aye Din bowed to the merchant and to the Sayadaw, promising to protect the gold until the merchant's return.

For many days Maung Aye Din tried to think of a way to keep the gold for himself without losing his hands to the great pincers. At last he thought of a clever plan. First he carved a hollow space in his walking staff. Then, melting the gold, he poured it into the hollow and sealed it all with wax.

Several months later, the merchant returned to the monastery and asked for his *viss* of gold. The Sayadaw called Maung Aye Din to his audience chamber, asking him to bring with him the merchant's gold.

"But, Venerable One, I have already returned the *viss* of gold to this noble merchant," Maung Aye Din exclaimed, pretending to be astonished at the request.

"Indeed he has not!" retorted the merchant. "I demand that my claim be heard by the high court." And with that the angry merchant strode away.

The next day, Maung Aye Din and the merchant appeared at the pagoda and stood before the judge. A great crowd had gathered, as it had been many months since the great pincers had been asked to settle a dispute. The merchant, who was the plaintiff, was first to make his statement. Placing his hands between the pincers, he called out loudly, "I gave one *viss* of gold to this Pongyi, requesting him to be steward of it while I was away. Now, I say he has not returned my gold to me."

The crowd watched anxiously to see what would happen next. But not a breath of movement did the great pincers make. Next it was the novice's turn. A murmur, like the rushing of water, flowed through the crowd, for if the merchant's statement was true, then the novice, a holy man to be, must be lying. Gravely, Maung Aye Din marched up to the pincers. He turned to the merchant, and holding out his staff, asked, "Will you hold this staff for me, friend?" The merchant nodded and took the staff. Then Maung Aye Din placed his hands between the great pincers. He bowed to the judge and to the merchant, then turning to the crowd, he cried in a loud voice.

"It is true that this merchant entrusted his *viss* of gold to me. I say that I have kept it safely. Further, I say I have returned the gold. He holds it now."

Not a sound could be heard as the crowd waited. But the pincers did not move. Suddenly the crowd burst into a roar. Surely one of the two men must be lying, but the pincers had allowed both to go unpunished. The crowd jeered and shouted. "The pincers are useless, the pincers lie!" they cried.

That night, the Sayadaw, being a wise old soul, called the novice to his chambers and demanded to see the walking stick. Of course he quickly found the gold, and returned it to the merchant the next morning. And the novice was shamed and driven from the kingdom for his base deed. But the wonderful pincers were so wounded by the jeers and the lack of faith of people of Pagan that they never again moved or pinched off anyone's hands, not even when some fool challenged them with outrageous statements or blatant lies.

The Fisherman
and the Gatekeeper

The ancient Mon city of Thaton stood near the mouth of the Salween river, and was the center of a highly developed civilization as early as 300 B.C., more than a thousand years before Pagan's rise to glory. And according to legend, it was the Mons who laid the earliest foundation stone for the great Shwedagon pagoda even earlier than that.

This tale is set near the sea, but no city is named in the original. Yet the quiet cleverness of the devoted fisherman is more characteristic of Burman than Mon stories, and this fisherman is certainly admired—probably reflecting a pre-Buddhist attitude.

Tun Win, the fisherman, lived not far from the great Mon city of Thaton. His father had been a fisherman before him, as had his father's father and his father's father's father. Now, the King of Thaton was planning a great banquet to celebrate the birth of his son and heir, offspring of his favorite wife, Queen Pyinsada. Ministers and lords from every corner of the kingdom were invited, and throughout the land there was great rejoicing.

Everyone was busy. Silversmiths made exquisite new bowls. Gold-workers pounded more gold leaf for the pagodas and images. Jewelers set emeralds and rubies into broaches and chains. Silk-weavers wove bolts of shimmering cloth with intricate designs, and merchants of every sort prepared their finest wares.

And, of course, much food would be needed. Paddygrowers set aside their whitest rice. Farmers chose their freshest vegetables and greens for the many *hins* (sauces and curries) that would be prepared. Fruit-pickers went far into the forest to find the ripest, plumpest fruits. And pastry cooks pounded rice flour and bought many jars of jaggery (palm sugar) to make hundreds of cakes and sweets.

But the main, and finest, course of the feast was to be steamed fish in a delicate sauce prepared by the King's chief cook. All the fishermen waited expectantly for the great day itself, for only the very freshest of fish would do. At last, the guests began to arrive from their distant cities and villages. They were taken to the many fine cottages the King had prepared for them, where they could spend the night in comfort and rest from their journeys.

However, the night before the great feast itself, a fierce storm blew from the south. Black clouds billowed over the sea, and white-crested waves pounded angrily against the rocks. Sadly, the King watched the storm from his tower. No fisherman would dare to brave that storm, and his wonderful feast would be spoiled. But when dawn came, Tun Win the fisherman appeared at the kitchen door hauling a large basket filled with the finest, fattest, freshest fish anyone could possibly desire. At once, the chief cook sent a message to the King that one brave fisherman had saved the feast. Greatly pleased, the King himself rushed into the kitchen. Tun Win *shikoed,* and all the cooks bowed reverently.

"You are a very brave young man," the King told the fisherman. "You could very well have been a dead one. Do you know that?" he asked.

Tun Win rose to his knees. "Yes, Sire. I knew there was danger. But a Prince has been born, and we all rejoice. It was worth risking my life for this celebration."

The King was very impressed. "Good fisherman," he said, "ask for anything you wish, up to one half of my kingdom, as a reward for your bravery."

"I thank you, Sire. I wish nothing except to be given one hundred firm lashes of a horse hair whip across my back."

The King frowned and cupped his ears. Surely he had not heard right. "Did you say you wished one hundred fine horses from my stable? I will give them gladly. That is a very small reward for your good deed. You may have one hundred elephants as well, if you so desire."

Tun Win shook his head and spoke again. "Sire, I asked only to be given one hundred whip lashes. I desire no other reward."

The puzzled King reamed his ears with his fingers. "Good fisherman, would you not prefer one hundred rubies the color of pigeon blood, or one hundred *viss* of gold, which you can use for many purposes?"

"No, Your Majesty. Thank you again for your generous offer. But my desire is to be granted one hundred strokes of the black whip. Please give me my reward as you promised."

The King shook his head in bewilderment. "So be it," he said. "Either this young fisherman is a fool, or he has made some religious vow," he thought to himself. "But a King must keep his promises."

So, summoning the Master of the Guard, the King gave orders for the young fisherman to be whipped. "But allow no stoke to bite through his flesh or cause him any harm," the King instructed. Then he departed, for he could not bear to witness this strange reward.

Tun Win bent silently to receive the lashes, but when fifty

strokes had been dealt, the young man called "Wait!" The startled guard waited. "The next fifty strokes belong to my Lord Chamberlain, Keeper of the Gate," Tun Win called out.

A great buzz arose and it was decided that the King must return to decide what must be done. "First one strange request, and now a second even stranger one," the King said. "What is your explanation?"

"Sire," replied the fisherman, "when I arrived at your palace gate early this morning with the fresh fish for your banquet, the Lord Chamberlain stopped me. He demanded half of any reward you offered. I did not wish to delay bringing you the fish, so I gave my promise. I have received my half of the reward. The other half now belongs to your Chamberlain."

The furious King summoned his Chamberlain who had no choice but to admit his avarice and receive his half of the reward. But this time the whip bit harshly, and the greedy gatekeeper was then banished from the kingdom.

The clever, brave youth, on the other hand, was appointed to a high position among the King's ministers, and served the King well all the rest of his days.

The Clever Boatman

In the original tale only the Irrawaddy is named, but traders regularly ply the wide Irrawaddy from Myitkyina (Myit-chen-ah) at the foot of the Himalayas, to Bassein or Yangon (Rangoon) in the extensive Irrawaddy delta. The ancient antagonism between the Burmans and the various ethnic groups who occupy the hills complicates Burma's present attempt to create a cohesive modern "Union of Burma." The boat master's scorn for the youth from the hills is turned upside down with a healthy laugh at the egotistical, conniving boat master.

There was once a youth named Lu Chin who lived in the northeastern hills of Burma. "Mother," he said one day, "tomorrow I shall go to Myitkyina and become a boatman on the great Irrawaddy. There I shall earn many kyat to buy you fine things, and soon, enough to support a wife and family of my own."

"As you will, my son," said his mother, "but keep your wits about you. You are strong and clever, but many will try to cheat you." And with that the mother bid her son farewell.

Within a few days, Lu Chin found a master of seven boats who was in need of another boatman and who hired the youth at once. The boat master, a greedy merchant from Mandalay, often hired hill men. Their life in the hills made them strong and hardy. Besides he could hire them for somewhat lower wages.

That night, as all the boatmen sat together sharing their supper, one friendly old fellow took Lu Chin aside. "As you know," he said, "by contract, the master will supply our food for the journey and a small stipend to spend along the way.

But not until we return to Myitkyina three months hence will we receive our wages. Do not under any circumstances bet with him. He considers himself a very clever fellow and thinks us hill men all a dull-witted lot. Often he has tricked a new man out of his entire wages for the journey!"

"Thank you, friend," said Lu Chin. "I shall be careful."

For many weeks the boats traveled down the river carrying their loads of fine *dahs* and baskets, earthen pots and jars of honey, and many sacks of rice to sell. At last they reached Yangon, where the boat master sold all the goods for a fine profit.

"What a wonderful place is this Yangon," Lu Chin said to himself as he wandered through the bazaar admiring silks and spices, tooled leathers, bronze gongs, and hammered silver bowls.

At a jewelers stall he spied a lovely filigree neck chain set with small pink spinel. "I will buy this one gift for my mother," thought Lu Chin, "but save all the rest of my wages. In a few years, perhaps I, too, can become a boat master."

The trip back up the Irrawaddy was long and slow. It was often necessary to walk along the bank, towing each boat. At each village and town, the boat master continued his profitable trades, while any boatmen who were not on watch would join in the local pagoda festivals, as it was the month of Pyatho.

On the last night of the journey, the boat master came over to the boatmen who had just finished their evening meal.

"Well, tomorrow you will all be wealthy, for you will receive your wages. Still, I wonder if any among you would like the chance to win all my boats from me? I am getting older, and perhaps it is time for me to sit home with my family."

The old boatman who had been a good friend to Lu Chin throughout the journey shot a warning glance at the youth, but Lu Chin ignored it.

"I wonder," continued the boat master, "if there is anyone here hardy enough to stay in the icy water the entire night, totally naked. If such a fellow succeeds, all my boats will be his, but if he leaves the water or otherwise warms himself before the sun rises, he will forfeit all his wages."

Lu Chin remembered the icy water in the streams at home and how he had often bathed in them. "I could win such a bet," he thought. "Then I will be a boat master much sooner than I dared to dream."

Lu Chin stood up. "I accept your challenge," he told the cunning boat master, even though he saw the old boatman shaking his head in warning.

"Then," said the boat master, "you boatmen must put out your night fire, for it would not be fair if this young fellow were to warm himself from its glow. Here are some extra blankets for you in its stead."

The boatmen put out their brazier while Lu Chin stripped and slid into the icy river. His teeth chattered and his body ached with the chill, but Lu Chin bravely stayed in the cold water. Just before dawn, some fishermen on the far bank of the river rose and lit a fire to prepare their morning food. Of course, the boat master had counted on exactly this to happen. He went to the side of the boat and began to scold. "You are cheating," he cried. "You are warming yourself by the fishermen's fire. You lose the bet. All your wages are mine."

"But," protested Lu Chin, "Their fire is nearly half a mile away. How can I possibly be warming myself by it?"

"A fire is a fire," retorted the boat master. "If you can see it, you are receiving the benefit of its warmth." Without further complaint, Lu Chin pulled himself from the icy river, wrapped himself in a warm blanket, and sat to enjoy breakfast with his fellow boatmen.

"Our boat master is not so clever as he thinks," Lu Chin chattered amiably. The others turned to him, astonished. They had expected him to mope and grumble.

"But he has just won all your three months' wages," said his older friend.

"True," said Lu Chin. "But I am certain he is not clever enough to roast pigs' feet. I bought some at the last village and was bringing them home. Only hill men really know how to roast pigs' feet properly."

The boat master, overhearing the youth's cheerful bragging, came over to the little group. "What a foolish idea that only hill men know how to roast pigs' feet. Of course I know how!"

"Are you willing to bet your fleet of boats once again?" asked Lu Chin.

"Of course," said the boat master. "And will you forfeit the next journey's wages as well, if I win this bet, too?"

Lu Chin agreed, and the boat master, eager to win more free labor, immediately accepted the wager. "Bring your pigs' trotters then, and you other fellows start a fire," he ordered.

"Oh, but you must use that fire," objected Lu Chin, pointing to the fishermen on the far side of the river.

"How can I possibly roast pigs' feet on a fire half a mile away?" protested the boat master.

"It was enough to warm me," answered Lu Chin. "Surely you can use it to roast the pigs' feet." At that all the boatmen laughed heartily.

Shamefaced, the master had to agree that Lu Chin had won, and the youth returned to his mother with the fine necklace and the boat master's fleet.

From that time on, Lu Chin hired young, strong boatmen from the hills each year, but he never tried to cheat anyone—boatman or merchant.

For an excellent retelling of another boatman story, read "Shan's Lucky Knife," by Jean Merrell (see Bibliography).

The Origin of the Coconut

The three preceding stories were about cleverness, but this one is about a prankster and the harm such people can sometimes do.

Once, a very long time ago, a raft carrying three people drifted to shore near the mouth of the great Irrawaddy River. The three were promptly taken before the King, who looked them over carefully and asked them many questions. He soon learned that each one of them had been exiled from a country across the seas after being accused of certain crimes.

"And what was this crime?" asked the King.

The first person admitted he had been caught stealing fish from a vendor. So the King gave him a house and a thousand pieces of silver and bade him welcome. "He was only a thief because he was poor and hungry," explained the King. "Now that he is not poor, he will make a good citizen."

The second person was a witch. She had been accused of making mice appear in her neighbors' rice baskets and enchanting snakes to make them steal mangoes from the neighbors' trees. To her, the King also gave a house and a thousand gold pieces and welcomed her to the country.

"This woman practiced witchcraft only because poverty left her hungry and ashamed. She envied her more fortunate neighbors with their full rice baskets and fine clothes. Now she will have money to buy food and good silk longyis, so she will no longer have any reason to be jealous. She, too, will make a good citizen."

Then the King questioned the third castaway, who

laughed and joked the whole time, finally admitting he had been exiled because of the mischief he had made among his neighbors by his pranks and lies and gossip.

"Take this man away at once," ordered the King, "and cut off his head. For, once a mischief maker, always a mischief maker. So long as this man is alive, he will harm others with his cruel games and tittle-tattle."

The prankster was promptly led to the execution block, and his head was severed from his body.

The next morning an officer passing by the execution block was surprised to see the head of the mischief-maker rolling about on the ground, laughing and joking. The officer was still more astonished when the head looked directly at him, opened his mouth and demanded, "Tell the King to come at once and bow before me. And if he will not come, I shall go to him and bash his head in."

The alarmed officer hurried to tell the King what he had just seen. The story was so unbelievable that the King, assuming the officer was trying to make a fool of him, started to order the officer to be whipped for his disrespectful behavior.

"But, Sire," the young officer pleaded, "if you will only send another officer with me, he can report that what I say is true." The King agreed and the two officers returned to the place of execution.

There, indeed, lay the head of the mischief-maker, but it neither spoke nor moved. When the second officer made his report, the King ordered the first man beheaded as a liar.

The King called all his officers to attend the execution so they might witness the fruit of falsehood. While the whole regiment watched, the first officer was beheaded, but no sooner had the blade completed its task when the head of the mischief-maker began to roar with laughter.

"Ha, ha, ha," he shouted. "Though I am dead, I can still make mischief with my tittle-tattle."

The anguished King, seeing the terrible mistake he had just made, ordered his guards to bury the head of the mischief-maker in a deep hole, for now he knew that even in death this scoundrel would always make mischief.

The next morning, to everyone's astonishment, a strange tall tree stood where the head had been buried. Its fruit so resembled the head of the mischief-maker, that the tree was called *gon-bin* or mischief-maker tree.

Over the years the name gradually became *on-bin,* or coconut tree. But if you shake the fruit and hold it close to your ear, you can hear a soft slurp and gurgle as the fruit continues to this day to try to make mischief with its tittle-tattle.

The Four Foolish Brothers

Nearly every land has stories about noodleheads, poking fun at those who follow directions too literally.

There were once four brothers who were so foolish that they seemed unable to do the simplest of tasks. The village wives often gave them rice out of kindness and sent them on their way, but as the brothers knew that most men worked for their living, they kept trying to find honest employment.

One day they met an old woman trudging through the fields carrying a heavy bundle of thatch. "Mistress, we are in need of work," said the oldest brother. "Do you have any task we could do in exchange for our dinner?"

The old woman looked at the four strong young men and immediately hired them to carry the remaining thatch for her. Promptly, the four went into the field where each brother picked up a large bundle and followed the woman to her house.

"Mistress, where shall I put this bundle of thatch," asked the first brother.

"Put it behind the kitchen," the woman replied, pointing to the spot.

The second brother coming right behind had heard the question and answer. Nevertheless, he too asked, "Mistress, where shall I put this bundle of thatch?"

"Put it behind the kitchen," the woman answered again, and the young man placed his bundle beside the first one.

The third brother had also heard, but he too asked, "Mistress, where shall I put this bundle of thatch?"

The woman sighed in annoyance but again said, "Put it behind the kitchen."

The last brother asked the same question and received the same answer. Then the four went to the field for more thatch. Each time a brother brought a bundle, he would repeat the same question, and all through the morning the old woman kept answering, "Behind the kitchen. Behind the kitchen."

After a while, she made herself a brew of tea to calm her nerves, but when for the fortieth time one of the brothers asked, "Mistress, where shall I put this bundle of thatch," her patience broke.

Exasperated, she shouted, "You fools, where do you think you should put the thatch? Put it on my head, of course!"

The four brothers, startled by her anger, all tossed their bundles into the air, aiming for the old woman's head. The bundles landed with such a thump that the old woman fell down dead, but the foolish brothers just headed back for more thatch as if nothing had happened.

A neighbor, watching this, roused all the village. The brothers were scolded and thrashed soundly, much to their amazement. Then the headman gave them an ax and sent them off to cut down a tree for the poor old lady's coffin.

The brothers meandered along the road, bewildered and still hungry. After a while, they came to a large tree. "Do you think this tree is big enough?" asked the oldest brother.

"Yes," said the two middle brothers.

"Good," said the youngest. "Then I will climb to the top so my weight will help it fall."

"We will help, too," said the middle brothers. "We will lean against the tree so that when it falls, it will land on our shoulders. That way we shall save ourselves the effort of having to lift it again.

So the first brother began to chop, the second and third brothers leaned against the tree, while the fourth brother climbed quickly to the top. After a time the tree fell, crushing the two middle brothers. Luckily, the fourth brother, who had been high in the branches, was only stunned by the fall.

The oldest brother went over to the others and asked "Brothers, are you dead or just sleeping?" Of course the brothers did not answer, so the first brother sat down to wait. In an hour or two the youngest brother recovered and sat up.

"I am glad you are awake," said the first brother. "I am hungry. We should go find some food, but our brothers are still asleep," and he pointed to the two who lay crushed under the weight of the tree.

Several days later a woodcutter passed by, driving his bullock cart. He noticed the two brothers sitting calmly beside the road near the two dead bodies. The woodcutter stopped and asked, "Do you need help?"

"No, thank you, sir," said the oldest brother. "We are just waiting for our brothers to wake up. But they are very lazy and only seem to want to sleep."

The woodcutter came closer, holding his nose. "You fools," he said. "Those two are not asleep. They are quite dead. Do you not recognize the foul smell of rotting flesh?" And he drove away.

The oldest brother stood up. "The woodcutter must be correct," he said, "for he seems a clever fellow. Let us go on." The youngest brother agreed, so the two started down the road together.

As neither man had eaten for several days, their stomachs were bloated and rumbling. Soon the youngest brother belched out some gas.

"What a foul odor," said the oldest brother. "You must be dead."

"That's true," said the youngest brother, so he lay down right there in the middle of the road.

The oldest brother walked on a few more steps. Then he, too, belched.

"Oh, Brother, that is indeed a foul odor," the youngest brother called from his place in the road. "I believe you must be dead too. Join me and we can keep each other company." So the two foolish brothers lay side by side in the road.

Soon a group of elephants came down the road hauling teak logs. "Get out of the road, you fools," called the chief Oozie.

"Sir, how can we get out of the road? We are dead," one brother called out.

"Dead indeed! I'll soon bring you to life," shouted the angry Oozie and he jumped from the elephant's neck and began to jab the brothers' legs with his driving spear. The brothers promptly jumped up yelping in pain.

"Your spear must possess great magic," said the oldest brother greatly awed. "It has returned us to life, just as you promised! Will you trade it for this ax?"

As the ax was more valuable than the spear, the Oozie agreed, and the brothers marched off, extremely pleased with themselves.

By now the brothers were very hungry indeed, so they went to the next town to seek work. On the way they passed a house where many people stood about lamenting and bringing flowers.

When the brothers inquired what had happened, they learned that this was the home of a rich man whose only daughter had just died. The oldest brother ran up to the desolate father crying, "Good sir, we can restore your daughter to life! Give us a few minutes alone with her and you shall see for yourself."

When the brothers were alone with the dead girl, they began to prod her legs with the driving stick they had obtained from the Oozie, but of course nothing happened. "Try harder, brother," said the youngest. So the older brother jabbed the girl in the arms, then the stomach, and finally even about her head, but the girl did not get up.

Soon the father came in, and seeing his beautiful daughter cut and mutilated, he flew into a fury and beat the brothers roundly.

"Why did you harm my daughter, even in death?" he asked through his tears.

"Good sir, we only wanted to please you so you would give us some food," they answered. By now it was clear that the brothers were only two simple fellows and could not understand what they had done.

"Young men," said the father, "you should have shed tears with us and called out, 'Oh Sister, Why have you left us? We mourn and sorrow for you.'" Then the father gave them each a bowl of rice and allowed them to go on their way.

Soon they passed a house where a wedding feast was being held. The brothers rushed up to the bride, pulled her from the table, and began weeping. "Oh Sister, why have you left us? We mourn and sorrow for you," they cried.

This caused a great commotion, and the bride's relatives grabbed the foolish brothers and beat them soundly. Bewildered, the foolish brothers apologized for upsetting things. "We only wanted to please you so you would give us a little food," explained the oldest brother.

The bride's relatives finally realized that these were only two foolish fellows who could not help their ignorance.

"You should have danced and sung and said how happy you were for us," said the groom. Then he gave the brothers some honey cakes and let them go on their way.

The brothers walked on until they came to a house where they heard loud shouting. Peering in the window, they saw a man and his wife yelling insults and beating each other with pans and sticks. Immediately the brothers rushed in. They began to dance and sing merry songs. Then the oldest brother shouted, "We are very happy for you both!" The startled couple at once stopped quarreling and began to beat the two brothers roundly.

"We only wanted to please you so you would give us some food," explained the oldest brother.

At that the couple realized that these were only two foolish fellows who could not help their ignorance. "You should have separated us and said, 'Curb your anger. Remember you are man and wife.'" Then they handed the brothers some fruit and allowed them to go on their way.

The brothers continued on down the road until they came to a field where they saw two large buffaloes bellowing and goring each other with their great horns. Immediately the brothers rushed in between the angry animals, shouting, "Curb your anger. Remember you are man and wife."

The buffaloes charged again, goring the brothers to death. And that was the end of the four foolish brothers.

❧

Part III: Wise Judges and Fair Decisions

Law Tales and An-ah-deh

In Burma, village life had little to do with kings and conquests. Typically a group of five villages formed a "circle," or governing unit. A respected elder's, or judge's, chief duty was to "restore harmony." When a dispute was brought to a judge, it was expected that all parties would leave satisfied—unlike our Western adversarial law where one contestant wins and the other loses.

This tradition is nourished by a special group of stories known as "Law Tales." From early childhood, villagers heard and admired Solomon-like solutions to various dilemmas. The stories formed a primer in fairness and common sense, which guided both the elders and villagers alike. The stories were also fun! The judge might be a talking animal such as Golden Rabbit or the beloved (non-historical) Princess Learned-in-the-Law but the decision would always be both clever and fair.

This regard for one another's feelings was evident in Burman custom even before the precepts of Buddhism were adopted. Perhaps nothing shows this more than "An-ah-deh," the art of never saying "No," and never putting anyone else into a situation where they would need to. It is a delicate balance of round-about questions so that neither person will "lose face" or feel challenged.

For example, when a young man decides he has found his future wife, he must manage to ask without requiring any answer until it is clear that both the girl and her parents would say yes. This starts by bringing the gift of a live chicken. If the future mother-in-law not only accepts the gift, but then invites the young man to dinner for the following night, he knows he may continue his quest.

The Just Price

What is a fair price for the mouth-watering smells of freshly fried fish? The wise and clever Princess Learned-in-the-Law settles a dispute between a greedy stall-keeper and a poor traveler.

Poor old U San Ba trudged along the hot dusty road on his way to visit his daughter and grandchildren in a distant village. At noon, he paused to sit in the shade of a padauk tree, where he spread his mat to rest his weary bones.

Under the very next tree, a woman had set up a wayside stall. She was frying fish and rice cakes to sell to passing travelers, but so far that day she had not had many customers.

The woman peered intently at U San Ba as he quietly unwrapped the palm leaf bundle he had brought with him and began eating his noon meal of boiled rice and vegetables. Her narrowed eyes seemed to count each morsel that disappeared into the old man's mouth, but U San Ba paid her no heed. However, the moment he had finished the last mouthful, the woman marched over to him, held out her hand, and demanded a silver coin for the fried fish.

"Old woman, whatever are you talking about?" San Ba asked, looking up astonished. "My meal was of rice and vegetables, which I prepared myself this very morning. I ate no fish or meat, and certainly none of yours."

"He cheats, he cheats," shouted the woman for everyone to hear. "His rice was flavored with the excellent odors of my fish, without which it would surely have been less tasty. He should pay for the smell of my fish."

The crowd that was gathering around was puzzled. The

old man had indeed eaten only the food he had brought with him. But on the other hand, it was true that the wind had been blowing from the north, carrying the fine aroma of the frying fish. Was not the woman correct in assuming that good odors add to good flavor?

When, after a time, the quarrel was still not resolved, the two went to ask the Princess Learned-in-the-Law to judge the case. After listening with care, the princess proclaimed the following:

"The stall-keeper says correctly that U San Ba enjoyed the smell of her fried fish as he ate. And U San Ba cannot deny that the wind did carry the good smell to his nose as he sat eating. Therefore, the old man must pay the price.

"The woman says her price for a plate of fish is one silver coin. Therefore, let the two go out into the courtyard and stand in the sunlight. Let U San Ba hold out a silver coin and let the woman take the shadow cast by that coin. For if the price of a plate of fish is a silver coin, then the price for the smell of that fish shall be the shadow of that coin."

The Cambodians have a similar story in which a greedy man tries to charge an old pongyi *for resting in the shade of his ox. The judge decides that the price of the shade is the shadow of a coin.*

The Wisdom of Mahauthada

Maha is a religious term meaning "great." Stories of Mahauthada are part of Buddhist holy writings that are studied and beloved in Burma. They should be given the same respect Jews, Christians, and Moslems reserve for Bible stories of Noah, Jonah, Moses, King David, and others. The following are only a few of many told about the young sage. The stories originated in Northern India, along with many other tales that arrived with Buddism.

There was once a wonderful child who was born in the kingdom of Mithila. The King's astrologers had predicted that one of the thousand male infants born on a particular day was to be "a bright flame" in their midst. From his earliest days, the child showed exceptional wisdom and performed miracles of healing, so that he soon became known as Mahauthada, the Great Remedy.

When Mahauthada reached the age of seven, his father, a rich merchant, built a great pleasure garden and invited all his son's birth-mates to live there with him. The young child himself planned and directed the construction of a marvelous play palace in the garden. Word of this unusual feat reached the ears of King Vedeha who, recalling the prophecy, wished to have the child brought at once to his court. But Thaynaka, the King's chief counselor, fearing for his privileged position, urged the King to first set certain riddles and difficult tasks for the child to solve. That way, he said, the King would know whether this child was indeed the prophesied "great flame."

Accordingly, the King sent a messenger with one enigma after another, which the child easily solved. But each time, the jealous Thaynaka said it was not enough proof and urged the King to set a still more difficult task.

The King possessed a magnificent emerald that had once hung from a fine flaxen thread. However, that thread had rotted with age and broken. Wishing to wear his fine gem once more, the King ordered his finest jewelers to restring it, but none knew how to remove the old thread without endangering the stone.

"Perhaps the young pundit can find a way," Thaynaka suggested, thinking that the child would surely fail. Accordingly, King Vedeha sent a messenger with the stone to Mahauthada. The child only smiled and said, "Bring me a strand of strong fine wool and a jar of honey. The King shall have his wish."

Mahauthada smeared honey on one end of the emerald and also on part of the woolen thread. Then, he pushed the sweetened thread a short way into the hole and placed the jewel over the opening of an ant's nest.

Eager for the honey, the ants at once crowded into the hole, devouring the rotten thread as they went. When they reached the honeyed wool, they began to tug and pull, hoping to store honey—thread and all—in their nest. Soon the fine new thread was drawn clear through. Mahauthada snipped off the honeyed end as a reward for the ants, and returned the newly-threaded emerald to the messenger.

The delighted King was eager for the child to be brought to the palace at once. But again, Thaynaka protested that more proof was needed. After a few more days, King Vedeha thought of a truly impossible task. "Yes, yes," agreed Thaynaka, certain the child would fail. The King sent his herald to the town where Mahauthada lived.

"Hear, oh people of Mithila. There is a certain swing in the palace garden in which the King delights," the herald announced. "But the rope has broken. He requires you to make him a new rope, using only the finest white sand. If it is not ready in fifteen days, you must pay a fine of one thousand silver coins." The worried townspeople consulted together.

"We all know that such a rope is not possible," said the chief ropemaker, "yet where can we obtain the thousand pieces of silver to pay the fine?"

"Perhaps Mahauthada can help," suggested an old grandmother. So everyone went to the garden where the child was playing with his 999 playmates.

When the child heard the problem, he frowned and thought awhile. "The King's riddle cannot be solved," he said at last. "Instead, we must give him an equally difficult puzzle." Then Mahauthada chose five ropemakers and explained what they must do and say.

On the fifth day, the ropemakers went to the palace and requested an audience. The King laughed as the five men *shikoed* before the throne, for he assumed the men had come to admit their failure.

"What, have you finished the rope so soon?" he mocked.

The oldest ropemaker lifted his head and spoke respectfully. "Sire, we have not yet begun for want of clear instructions. We do not know how long the rope is to be, or how thick or thin. Please send us a cubit of the old rope, so we can copy it exactly. Thus you will have your new rope within the time you require."

This time the King laughed heartily and with no malice. "Who taught you these clever words?" he asked. The old ropemaker replied that it was Mahauthada.

"It is just as I suspected," King Vedcha exclaimed, and he would be put off no longer. He summoned the child and all his 999 playmates, and proclaimed that the young pundit was to be his son and heir.

———

Soon after the youth came to live with the King, a new problem arose. One of the gardeners spied a large and beautiful ruby lying at the bottom of a pond, and called the head gardener to come see it. The old man, realizing its value, went at once to the King, asking what was to be done. In turn, the King called Thaynaka and asked, "What is the best way to retrieve the ruby?"

"Why, drain the pond," answered the chief counselor, annoyed that the King had bothered him with such a simple question. At once, the pond was emptied, but no ruby could be found, even though every gardener searched the mud for hours.

With the next rain, the pond filled again, and there, once more, the rich red glow of the ruby shone in the water. A second time, the gardener reported to the King who came to see for himself. And again, the King asked for Thaynaka's advice.

The counselor roundly scolded the gardeners for their sloth. "Drain the pond again," he ordered, "and this time search with diligence!"

Of course, for a second time, the gardeners emptied jar after jar from the pond, but no matter how carefully they searched, no ruby could be found. A third time, the pond filled with water, and a third time the ruby could be clearly seen in the water. This time the King called Mahauthada and explained what had occurred.

The boy looked at the red rays of the ruby shining at the bottom of the pond. Then he looked around the pond. Near the edge grew a tall palm tree, and the child could see that a crow had built her nest in the tree.

"There is no ruby in the pond," he said. Everyone gasped in astonishment.

"But surely it is," argued the King. "Only a ruby has such fine color."

"Bring me a ladle," Mahauthada ordered. Promptly a servant ran from the kitchen carrying a fine large ladle which the child dipped into the pond. "See," Mahauthada said.

"Now the ruby seems to be in this ladle, but it cannot be in both the ladle and the pond. You will find the ruby in the crow's nest up there. The sun's light casts its radiance into the pond, creating the illusion of the jewel. "

The old gardener ordered a *mahli* boy to climb the palm. Exactly as the young sage had predicted, the boy brought down a fine blood-red ruby as large as an egg.

Some time later, Mahauthada journeyed to a village in a neighboring country, where he visited at the home of one of his childhood friends. The King of this country, hearing that the people of this village were especially clever, decided to test them. He therefore sent his herald to the village with the following message:

"Oh, people of Taikkala, your King desires to bathe and row in a beautiful and wild forest lake, but his duties require him to stay close to the palace. As there are are several such lakes near your village, he calls on you to find one for him. It must be surrounded by many fruit and flowering trees, and must bloom with each of the five types of lotus. Bring it to him before sundown eight days hence, or pay a fine of one thousand *viss* of silver." The dismayed villagers hurried to Mahauthada and reported the King's strange command.

The young pundit just smiled. "Be calm, good people.

Send me five strong and clever young men, and your problem will be solved." When the youths arrived, Mahauthada explained what they must do.

"Go to the lake," he told them, "taking spears and slings and cudgels and a strong hauling rope. First you must rub these with mud. Then swim and play in the water until your eyes become red and sore and your hair and clothes drip with wetness. Next you must play at tug-of-war near the muddy shore, until both you and the rope are well smeared with mud. After that is accomplished, run to the eastern gate of the palace and seek an immediate audience with the King. When you are admitted, rush in with great urgency, and not with the customary slow and reverent manner." Then Mahauthada explained what words they must say.

The next day the youths did all Mahauthada had instructed. They arrived at the palace breathless and hot from running and were quickly brought before the King, where they *shikoed* deeply.

"Oh Sire, filled with Wisdom and Glory, Great Builder of Pagodas," said the eldest youth, "we have heeded your order to the people of Taikkala. This very day we proceeded into the jungle to obtain the lake you required. We soon subdued it, tied it with this rope, and lead it to the very edge of your Royal City.

"As to why we have come in such a disheveled and hurried manner, we must explain that this is a very wild lake. It has not seen throngs of people, nor walls and turrets, nor prancing horses pulling carriages. In terror, it began leaping and pulling until at last the rope broke and the lake started running back to the jungle. We gave chase, beating it with our cudgels, stoning it and threatening it with our spears, but such a wild and frightened lake was more than we could manage.

"Perhaps, if you will lend us the tame lake from the Royal Gardens, we can do as elephant drivers who must quiet a newly captured elephant calf. If we tie the quiet lake to the frightened wild one, we believe that we can calm it enough to bring it to you." Then the eldest youth *shikoed* once more and awaited the King's reply.

The King laughed heartily when he heard these words. "I have never heard of a wild lake tied with a rope and led through the jungle, and certainly not one harnessed, like a frightened wild elephant, to a tame one so it might be calmed.

With all my royal power I could not do such a thing. Nor could I have planned such a clever game as you have played on me this day. Is this your own cleverness, or has some pundit advised you."

The eldest youth replied, "Mahauthada stays in our village with a friend. The plan was his."

Again the King laughed. "Ask the young pundit to visit me at my palace before he returns to his own kingdom. I would like to meet such a clever man." Then the King dismissed the village youths with his blessings and a thousand pieces of silver, that they might share them with the poor.

Rope of Pearls, Round of Lies

The anonymous Princess Learned-in-the-Law appears in many Burmese stories, even though learning was usually the exclusive province of males—be they king or commoner. While a learned woman was rare, both history and legend tell of several royal women who became highly-skilled in the arts of reading and writing, and who studied the laws and the holy texts. One such woman was Shinsawbu, Queen of Pegu from A.D. 1453 to 1472, arbitrarily chosen for this retelling. In another version, it is a clever prime minister who unravels the mystery, true to the Jataka (thus Indian) origin of the tale.

There was once a beautiful and clever Princess named Shinsawbu. Her father, King Razadarit of Pegu, was a wise and beloved ruler who doted on his daughter, and as he had no son to succeed him, King Razadarit often allowed Shinsawbu to sit at his side when he received envoys. He allowed her to play in the royal gardens, her skirts tucked in a manner suited only to boys, clambering up trees and kicking her *chinlon* into the air with her royal playmates. Most alarming of all, King Razadarit permitted his daughter to be schooled in reading and writing, and even the laws and holy texts.

The old Ministers, who had served the King's father before him, shook their heads gravely over such an unseemly upbringing for a Princess and future Queen.

"Sire," the Prime Minister often said, "Females are not suited to learning. The Princess will misread the sacred texts and confuse the meaning of the laws and thus bring havoc on our land." But the King only replied that his daughter seemed to be an apt and eager pupil.

"But Sire," the Minister would continue, "one day your daughter will wed an important King, joining the two kingdoms. If your daughter deems herself learned, she will attempt to influence his opinions. Females cannot understand complex matters of state. She would thus weaken the kingdom."

But the King would reply, "Who would care more deeply for the welfare of our land, my daughter or some foreign Prince?" And to that the Ministers could give no answer. As it turned out, it was the Ministers who had much to learn.

The palace at Pegu was a place of great beauty. Its many apartments and rooms of state were high and airy. Latticework and delicate open-carved screens invited cool breezes and shade. In spite of the blistering sun, the palace grounds were green and fragrant, tended by a faithful old gardener who, like the Ministers, had also served at the palace for many long years.

The private apartments of the Princess included an especially beautiful garden. At one end, a tall jacaranda tree spilled lavender blossoms and cool shade across the pebbled ground. From the surrounding trees, jewel-colored pie-birds called, and small excited monkeys danced in the branches. Jasmine bushes filled the air with perfume. Roses framed one edge of a bathing pool where clear water rippled with every passing breeze. Upon the water, the sacred lotus bloomed in rare and delicate hues. The Princess was very safe in her garden, for thick planks of russet teak formed a strong wall to keep out thieves, knaves, and curious eyes. And at all times, two strong guards stood watch just outside the gate.

But there was one pair of curious eyes no one had noticed.

Each day, a little she-monkey would peer intently from her screen of leaves, watching the beautiful Princess and wishing to touch the pretty things she wore. The little animal was particularly attracted to an exquisite rope of pearls Shinsawbu constantly wore. Her father had presented them to her on her eighteenth birthday, and she treasured them above all her other jewels.

One hot April afternoon, the Princess went into her garden to bathe and cool herself. As usual, she removed her silks and ornaments and gave them to her little handmaiden, Ma Thein Tin, who laid them one by one on a white cloth. The child sat by, patiently waiting to help her mistress dry and dress. But this day, the late sun was especially fierce and the Princess lingered in the cool water. The child's head soon began to swim with heat and weariness, and she fell asleep.

The little monkey, seeing her chance, silently lowered herself from a vine and crept over to the cloth. Delicately, she put out a finger to caress a satiny globe. Suddenly, she grasped the whole rope of pearls, wound it around her neck, and skipped back into the tree. Then, worried that the other monkeys might notice her treasure and snatch it away, she hid the necklace in a hole in the jacaranda tree.

Ma Thein Tin soon awoke and saw the necklace was missing. Ashamed and fearful, the servant girl began to shout, "HELP! GUARDS! A thief has stolen my lady's necklace!" Though, of course, she had no idea what had really happened.

The guards burst into the garden and immediately began to beat the bushes and hunt high and low for the thief. The Princess, startled by all the commotion, quickly pulled her blue silk robe about her, stepped from the water, and beckoned the child to come stand by her. Together, they watched the guards search the garden.

The old gardener was hoeing under a mango tree just outside the garden gate. Frightened by the noise, he began to run and the guards, who were new to the palace, assumed he was the thief. At once they began to beat him, demanding the necklace.

The terrified old man protested that he had not stolen the pearls, but the guards did not believe him, and they beat him all the harder until he cried, "Yes, yes, I stole the jewels." Whereupon the guards dragged him away to the King.

Now this learned and perceptive daughter of King Razadarit realized that the old gardener could not have been inside the garden. She looked up at the chattering monkeys and surmised what had probably occurred. Cupping the child's chin in her hand, the Princess asked, "Did you actually see the man who stole my pearls?"

The girl tried to drop her head, but could only avert her eyes and answer softly, but truly, "No, Mistress. I fell asleep for a moment. But surely someone must have stolen them!"

"Perhaps!" said the Princess. "And I think we can find out. But, first, let us see what trouble you have made for the old gardener. I have watched him coax beauty from the black earth. I believe that old man finds beauty enough without stealing jewels. Such a deed might cost him his life, and certainly would cost him his job, which he does with such devotion."

Princess Shinsawbu dressed quickly, took Ma Thein Tin by the hand, and hurried to the King's audience room. But she did not go boldly to the royal seat beside her father's throne. Instead she and the child entered through a side door and sat behind the women's screen to watch through the lace of carved teak leaves and flowers.

They watched the guards enter, dragging the poor frightened old man between them. Then the guards threw the gardener down before the King, and prostrated themselves as well.

"Lord of the Sunrise," called the first guard, "This old man has stolen a rope of pearls from the Princess Shinsawbu's private garden."

"Is this true?" asked the astonished King, for he knew the old gardener well. When the dazed old man just nodded, King Razadarit spoke. "Give them to me immediately, then, that I may make matters right as quickly as possible."

"Sire," sobbed the old gardener, "I am a poor and humble man of no importance. I have no use for jewels. The blossoms of the earth are my treasure, as you yourself well know. I stole the pearls, but not for myself."

"Then for whom," demanded the King. "And where are they now?"

The old gardener looked about, confused. After a moment he murmured, "I gave them to the Prime Minister." But he would say no more.

"Is this so?" asked the puzzled King turning to the Prime Minister, who agreed that the old gardener had indeed brought him the rope of pearls.

"But, Sire," he said "I no longer have them. I gave them to the Royal Treasurer."

So the Royal Treasurer was summoned. "Yes," admitted the treasurer. "I did receive the rope of pearls, but I gave them to the Royal Jeweler. He is to prepare a matching chain of silver, onyz, and sapphire—a gift for the Princess's birthday."

"Yes," admitted the Jeweler when he was summoned. "The Treasurer did ask me to make such a chain. It is completed and I have given both it and the rope of pearls to the Royal Musician."

"Yes," admitted the Musician. "But Su Kyi, the singing girl, has it now. The Prime Minister asked me to compose a special song for her to sing at the birthday celebration before presenting the new jewels, after which, you, Sire, would return the rope of pearls to the Princess yourself."

"Rope of pearls? Silver chain set with sapphire?" answered the indignant Su Kyi. "I do not have them! It is true the Royal Musician and I have prepared a new song for the Princess's birthday, but I was given nothing! Nothing at all!"

King Razadarit shook his royal head and ordered the six to be locked together in the Prime Minister's private chambers for the night under under heavy guard.

"I will tell you my decision in the morning," he said sweeping away to his own chambers to think.

Silently, Princess Shinsawbu and little Thein Tin slipped from the throne room. *I am certain the King knows these stories cannot possibly be true,* she thought, *but who is lying, and why? I must find out.*

She turned to Ma Thein Tin. "Go quickly. Fetch some worn old servants' rags and a shawl, and bring them to me," she instructed. Soon, the Princess, disguised as an old charwoman, busied herself raking just beyond the Prime Minister's window.

"Wretch!" she heard the angry Minister exclaim, apparently addressing the old gardener. "Why did you steal the pearls and then blame me, you worthless old creature. Look at all the trouble you have caused!"

"Minister," the still bewildered old gardener said, "I did not steal the pearls, but the young new guards would not believe me. I feared their clubs would soon beat the life from me, so I confessed to what I did not do. Then, in my great fright, as I lay prostrate before the King, I thought of your wisdom and the King's trust in you. With you at my side, I hoped we could explain our innocence."

At this the Minister was wordless, while the Treasurer exclaimed in a loud petulant voice, "But, Minister, instead you blamed me! Where was your wit? Could you not have told the truth, or made some likely story?"

"Treasurer, you are too harsh!" the Prime Minister replied. "In saying the pearls were with you, I expected you could think of an explanation quickly. Your clever brain has often created fine stories, thus saving our King from much undue worry!"

"And I did so again!" the Treasurer answered crossly. "If the singing girl had not protested, we would have had five days to find the pearls or replace them, and have the new chain crafted. The King would have been content, and we would have had a fine birthday gift as well!"

Peering through the window from behind a rose trellis, the Princess could see the singing girl swing around in great anger to face the Jeweler and Musician.

"And you!" Su Kyi glowered at the Musician. "You took part in this great foolish pretense! Do you do so often?"

Soon everyone was speaking at once. All but the old gardener.

"The King should not be troubled with small matters!" exclaimed the Minister. "Of course we make stories. It is to protect him from the many worries of state."

The Treasurer, the Jeweler and the Musician all agreed, admitting they had always done this for King Razadarit, and for his father before him. The Princess could see the old gardener slouched in a corner, weeping at what he presumed he had started. Sadly, she returned to her apartment. By the time she arrived she had formed a plan, and Ma Thein Tin was eager and willing to help.

First the child ran to find one of the boys who helped in the gardens. "Princess Shinsawbu wishes you and the other boys to capture as many monkeys as you can and place them in bamboo cages for the night," she told them.

The boys were accustomed to stange requests from the Princess, and they set right to work skimming up the bamboos and trees outside the palace walls. Soon they had more than a dozen monkeys.

Next, Ma Thein Tin ran to the King's wardrobe keeper. "Princess Shinsawbu wishes you to go to the Royal Theater, collect many pieces of glittering false jewelry, especially ropes of beads, and bring them to her." The King's wardrobe-keeper was accustomed to strange requests from the Princess, and soon he arrived with several small chests filled with beads and baubles. Last of all, Ma Thein Tin hurried to the King's own chambers with a sealed letter from Princess Shinsawbu which she was to deliver into the King's own hands.

Early the next morning, boys and monkeys arrived at the Princess's garden gate. Ma Thein Tin woke the Princess, and informed her that they had arrived, then they stood together in the garden to watch what would happen next.

How the little animals chattered and squealed as the boys offered them beads and baubles and then released them. Screaming with delight, they scampered back into the trees, displaying their treasures, posturing and clicking their teeth in proud grins. The little she-monkey, who had taken the pearls, noticing her companions with glittering finery of their own, rushed to get the rope of pearls from the hole where she had hidden it.

One of the boys approached the little thief, dangling a strand of gaudy glass "emeralds" so that they sparkled and gleamed in the morning sunlight. The greedy creature, wanting these as well, riveted her attention on the newer, brighter treasure.

As she reached out to grab it, the boy deftly snatched the pearls. The monkey's dismay was only brief as she turned to admire her new prize. Ma Thein Tin laughed at the whole performance. Clearly, her lie had been forgiven. She would never again cover one mistake with another.

As for the others, King Razadarit summoned the six, and with his daughter at his side, read aloud a letter explaining all that she had discovered. In the end, the old gardener and the singing girl were returned to their duties. But the Ministers were banished from the land with harsh and bitter words for believing lies would serve their King.

And surely, the Ministers had much reason to regret that Princess Shinsawbu was learned in writing and the law.

The Measure of Rice

This time a greedy king fires his honest "valuer" and hires a fool instead. This is one of the Jataka tales, with a lesson to tell.

There was once a beautiful city filled with shining pagodas, prosperous shops, and many well-built houses. Wide shady streets and exquisite public gardens with restful ponds graced the city with fragrant blooms and quiet coves.

All this had come about because of the wise and peaceful reign of the young King's father and grandfather and their fathers before them. But this new young King was spoiled and greedy, and far from wise. People called him the Paw Gyi Min, or Great Simpleton, though certainly no one would dare call him that to his face!

Among the young King's many ministers was a man called the Valuer. It was his task to decree what prices would be paid for horses and elephants, bullocks and buffalo, or any other animals purchased for the King or the royal city. He also set the price on gold and jewels, delicate jade carvings, and fine porcelain vases.

He was a venerable old man who had served the young King's father before him. Over those many long years, he had set prices with such fairness and justice that much of the city's prosperity resulted directly from his honesty and wisdom. But the Paw Gyi Min kept thinking how much richer he would be if another sort of man was his Valuer.

Accordingly, the King dismissed his old Valuer, presenting him with a fine house in the cool hills, many miles away from the Royal City. This was presumably to honor him for his long, faithful service, but it would also keep the old man far from the Royal City, and prevent him from discovering Paw Gyi Min's plan.

There was at the palace an old gardener called U Nga Ah, or Uncle Stupid, who helped around the grounds doing small chores that required little understanding. The King recalled how the old man had often brought him little gifts of flowers, small turtles or *toc-toc* lizards when he was just a young Prince playing in the palace gardens. This was exactly the sort of Valuer the Paw Gyi Min wanted. The old gardener would be eager to please, and too simple to understand the real value of anything. So the King promptly appointed U Nga Ah the new Valuer.

At once, the old gardener put on his silk robes of office and hurried to the gilded kiosk beside the market. As he knew nothing of the customary value of anything, he said whatever came into his head and the tradespeople had to sell at whatever price he set.

Of course this caused much grumbling, for the former gardener set most prices too low. The King, however, flattered and honored him (and privately smiled as his wealth mounted.)

In response to this flattery, U Nga Ah set the prices lower and lower. Those who could, began to travel away seeking some other kingdom where they could trade and prosper under fair and honest rules. But most of the people could do nothing. They grew poorer and poorer while the King grew richer.

After some months, a horse-dealer arrived at the palace, bringing with him a string of five hundred fine horses captured in the great plains beyond the northern Snow Mountains. In past years the horse-dealer had traded with the King's father, and now expected to be well and honestly paid for his long effort. He knew nothing of what had happened since the young Paw Gyi Min had become King.

The horse-trader bowed deeply before the new Valuer and displayed some of his finest horses. Then he offered to take the Valuer to the stockade outside the city to inspect the rest.

Old U Nga Ah declined to go. Instead he smoothed his fine robes, thought of the King's approving smile and said, "Yes, yes. Fine horses indeed. Give this good trader a measure of rice."

The astonished trader could do nothing but accept the rice and watch his fine horses being led to the royal stables. Nevertheless, he made inquiries and soon learned all that had occurred since the death of the Paw Gyi Min's father.

Before the week was out, the trader rode to the cool blue hills to find the former Valuer. When he told him all that had been happening in the royal city, the old man rubbed his chin and thought awhile.

"I know that old gardener," he said at last. "He is dull-witted but kindly and only seeks to please his King. Take him an expensive gift and flatter him. I believe you can then make him say whatever you wish."

The two talked and planned and had a fine supper together. The next morning the trader returned to the city. At noon he went to the home of U Nga Ah taking with him an exquisite jade-and-silver vase filled with jasmine and roses, and a large carrier of steaming rice with little tins of excellent curries.

The trader bowed low and offered the gifts. "Saya," he said, "In your wisdom you allowed me to learn that a measure of rice is very valuable. It is equal to the five hundred horses I brought from the north. Share this good meal with me. It is the highest honor I can pay you for my new wisdom."

U Nga Ah was highly flattered, besides his stomach growled with hunger as the delicious smells filled the room. Eagerly, he accepted the trader's offer. As they ate, the gardener turned to admire the vase with its fresh, fragrant flowers.

"They are beautiful, are they not?" noted the trader.

"Yes, indeed," replied U Nga Ah.

"Saya, in your wisdom, which would you say is more valuable, this delicious meal or that vase and its flowers?" the trader asked.

"That is a difficult question," answered U Nga Ah, "for if I am hungry and have nothing to eat, the rice is more valuable. But if I am full, then for me it would be the flowers."

"Tell me then, Wise One," continued the trader, "how then would you value a house against this rice?"

"Ah! If it is night and I am cold, the house and the rice would be equal," decided the Valuer.

"And this Royal City?" asked the trader. "Is its value more or less than the value of a house?"

"What would I want with more than one house?" answered the Valuer. "Again they would be equal."

"Such wisdom! I am glad to learn from you," murmured the trader. "Would you come with me and say to the King what you have told me this night?"

"Gladly," replied the Valuer, more flattered than ever.

The next morning, the trader and the Valuer went to the court. Many guests and ministers had assembled. The former Valuer came too, but he had disguised himself as a poor farmer, and no one noticed. U Nga Ah and the trader bowed low before the King.

"Sire," began the Valuer, "last evening this excellent man and I dined together. Our conversation was most revealing. I thought I had but a humble mind, but now I see I have great wisdom and must share it with you, if you will permit."

"And what is this special wisdom?" asked the Paw Gyi Min.

"Sire," replied the Valuer. "I have discovered that this fine Royal City is equal in value to a measure of rice." And he continued to recount the conversation of the previous evening.

The King's face grew red with anger as the Valuer spoke, and the Ministers began to twitter, finally bursting into laughter. "We thought this fine city was priceless," they whispered behind their hands. "Now we discover it is worth only a measure of rice. What an empty-headed minister."

"—And what a stupid King to appoint such a man as royal Valuer," others added.

Looking about him, poor old U Nga Ah realized at last that everyone, was laughing at him—and that his beloved King was choked with fury.

"Out of my sight, you old fool," shouted the King. "You think like a child!"

With that, U Nga Ah ran weeping from the room, while the King, who had also overheard the ministers and guests, stalked off to his private chambers. In the end, the King reappointed his old Valuer, sent the gardener to the fine estate in the country, and paid the trader handsomely for the horses. As the years went by, he copied the ways of his father and grandfather before him and no one called him the Paw Gyi Min anymore. Instead he was called the Myint Tha Min, the Noble Better King, and this they were glad to say to his face.

The following year, the trader again brought fine horses, which he sold to the King at a fair price. That evening the old Valuer invited the trader to dine with him. "The sad thing is," said the trader, "the old gardener was correct as to the true worth of rice and shelter and flowers—though such prices would never suit in the market place."

The Case of the Calf and the Colt

Golden Rabbit is one of the most beloved characters in Burmese folk tales. He is almost always clever, sometimes wise, usually helpful, and occasionally cruel. Compare the Rabbit's behavior to that in "Shwe Yone and Shwe Kyae" in Part IV.

Once there were two neighbors. One man had come to be called Ko' Lu Taw, or Mr. Clever, because of his quick wit and clever tongue. The other man, though he was honest and dependable, was called Ko' Lu Ah, or Mr. Stupid, because of his quiet, plodding ways. Now it happened that Ko' Lu Taw owned a cow, while Ko' Lu Ah, in spite of his slow and simple ways, had come to own a mare. Both animals were pregnant and close to term.

One night, Ko' Lu Taw woke to hear the distressed bellowing of his cow as she began to give birth. Taking a lantern, he went to his barn to attend her. Soon he heard whinnies from his neighbor's barn as the mare, too, began giving birth. But everything in Ko' Lu Ah's stable remained dark, for the man was a sound sleeper.

This gave Ko' Lu Taw an idea. *Ko' Lu Ah is so dull witted I can surely fool him,* he decided. Leading the calf to his neighbor's stable, he placed it with the mare, then he led the colt away to his own barn.

The next morning, Ko' Lu Taw rose early and ran about the village in great excitement, telling of the wonder that had happened in the night. His cow had miraculously given birth to a colt!

All the neighbors rushed to Ko' Lu Taw's barn to behold this marvel. By now, Ko' Lu Ah had awakened and wandered sleepily into his stable. At first he was confused to see a calf standing beside his mare and wondered at the strange event. Then, hearing the commotion at his neighbor's house and words spoken about a miracle colt, he quickly surmised what had happened, for he was not so stupid as Ko' Lu Taw supposed.

He ran from his stable shouting angrily at Ko' Lu Taw. "You thieving villain! You have stolen my colt!"

But Ko' Lu Taw, still thinking he could easily confuse his dull-witted neighbor, declared that surely a second miracle must have happened, for behold, Ko' Lu Ah's mare had given birth to a calf on that same night of wonders.

Ko' Lu Ah stubbornly refused to believe his neighbor, and by now the villagers were divided over what indeed was the truth. A miracle would be something fine to boast about. And yet....

Finally, it was decided that Rabbit, wisest of all the animals, should be called, so the two men traveled to the forest. When Wise Rabbit heard their tale, he readily agreed to be their judge. "In seven days I will come to your village and give you my decision," he promised.

Accordingly, on the seventh day, Ko' Lu Ah and Ko' Lu Taw arrived at the village square dressed in their best silk *longyis* and jackets, jaunty *gaungbaungs* tied on their heads. Indeed, all the village had come in their finest—for they, too, were anxious to hear the judgment of Wise Rabbit.

The sun rose high above the eastern hills, but Wise Rabbit did not appear. Noon came, bringing the haze and heat of midday, but no Wise Rabbit. The dusty afternoon wore on, and still the people waited, hot and hungry.

At last, as the sun dipped low and the red dust turned

saffron in its rays, Judge Rabbit appeared, hot and out of breath.

"Are you all right?" asked an old man. "We feared some misfortune had befallen you."

Judge Rabbit looked sternly at the old man, for it is not seemly to question a judge. Nevertheless he answered, loudly enough for all to hear.

"Forgive my delay, good people. But you see, as I journeyed on my way this morning, I noticed a sandbar in the middle of the river that had caught fire. I have spent the entire day fetching water to quench it. As I had only a wicker crate in which to carry the water, it took quite some time."

The villagers all exchanged puzzled looks over these astonishing words, while Ko' Lu Taw frowned, wondering whether Wise Rabbit was testing him.

I will show Wise Rabbit that I am no fool, he thought at once. "Pardon, Sir Judge," he said, clasping his hands reverently, "but a sandbar in a river surely cannot burn, and water cannot be carried in a wicker crate. It is against the laws of nature."

"Congratulations!" said Wise Rabbit. "You are observant and quite right. It is indeed against the laws of nature. And so is a cow giving birth to a colt, or a mare giving birth to a calf. Thus, you will return your neighbor's colt and apologize for your deceit." And Wise Rabbit walked away amid the applause of the village. How cleverly he had demonstrated the truth and brought about justice.

Thereafter, Ko' Lu Taw was called Ko' Kauk Kway, or Mr. Crooked, while kindly old Ko' Lu Ah became Ko' Phaung Mat, or Mr. Straight, and was widely respected.

As for Wise Rabbit, from that time on the villagers always chose him as judge whenever there was a dispute between neighbors.

Part IV:
The Creatures of Jambudipa

Tricksters and Saints

A nimal tales in every culture fall roughly into three categories: (1) trickster stories told just for the fun of watching one animal outsmart another; (2) fables told to present a sugar-coated moral; and (3) "just so" stories to explain how it all began. In such stories the animals speak and act with human thoughts and motives, and what little is characteristic of their animal nature is just "costume."

The first story, "Shwe Yone and Shwe Kyae" ("Golden Rabbit and Golden Tiger") is only a trickster tale, while "The Shy Quilt Bird" and "The Magic Mango" include all three elements—clever tricks, "how it all began," and a moral as well.

"The Foolish Crocodile" probably began as a Jataka tale from India in which a clever monkey outsmarts the crocodile. In this distinctly Burman version, Golden Rabbit is once again the wise trickster.

There is no great paradox in including the *nat* stories with these animal tales. In Burman Buddhist cosmology, animals dwell only in the great southern island of Jambudipa while *nats, nagas, bilus,* ghosts and many other mythical beings inhabit the universe in general.

To the Burmans, such spirit creatures were as real as tigers, (rarely seen) and lions (never seen). Besides, many *nats* were reincarnated humans, at least according to the legends.

Shwe Yone and Shwe Kyae,
or Golden Rabbit and Golden Tiger

This time, Golden Rabbit is a cruel prankster, very pleased with his own cleverness. This story is a great favorite with children and adults alike!

Golden Rabbit and Golden Tiger had been good friends since the beginning of time. One day, while they were both building new houses, Golden Rabbit said, "Tiger, my friend, tomorrow, let us go to the fields together to gather thatch for our houses." Golden Tiger was pleased with the idea and agreed eagerly.

At dawn the next morning, Golden Tiger took his reaping knife from the shelf, prepared a fine meal of rice and some curry which he wrapped in a palm leaf packet, and set off to meet Rabbit.

Golden Rabbit was already waiting. He too had brought his reaping knife and a packet. But Rabbit's packet was not filled with food. It contained clay and sand and some twigs.

"Good morning, Friend Tiger," Golden Rabbit said, grinning to himself as he thought of the clever tricks he had planned. "What a fine morning we have for gathering thatch."

The two walked along the river road, through the groves and orchards to the thatch fields. They stopped only a few minutes to cut some liana vines which they would need for binding the thatch into bundles. When they got to the thatch field, Golden Rabbit said, "Tiger, my friend, I feel faint from our long walk. Let us eat something before we work." But Tiger, who was always diligent, was eager to begin work immediately.

"Do rest, Friend Rabbit," Tiger said sympathetically, "and perhaps you should eat a little of your food. Then, when you feel stronger you can join me."

Rabbit flopped under a bush and gazed gratefully at Tiger. "Are you sure you will not rest awhile and eat with me before you work?" he asked. "I have heard it said: 'He who eats early gets rice for the day, but he who eats late receives dry sand and clay!'"

"I thought the word was 'commences,' not 'eats,'" said Tiger with a good-natured chuckle. And he turned to go into the field to work.

As soon as Tiger was out of sight, Rabbit laughed aloud, thinking of the clever tricks he had planned. Quickly he ate all of Tiger's delicious dinner and lay back in the shade to plot more mischief.

At noon, Golden Tiger returned with a fine bundle of thatch. His poor stomach growled hungrily, but when he opened his food packet, it contained nothing but clay and sand and some twigs. Angrily, Tiger flung down the packet. "Where is my dinner?" he demanded. "Did you eat that, too?"

"Of course not!" Rabbit lied, sounding terribly hurt. "Allow me to see."

Golden Rabbit looked at the contents of Tiger's palm leaf and feigned great surprise. "Perhaps the saying really is true after all," he said, and he again chanted: "'He who eats early has rice for the day, but he who eats late receives dry sand and clay!'"

The bewildered Tiger, who was not very clever, apologized to Golden Rabbit for doubting him. He chewed on a handful of sweet grass, but his empty stomach continued to growl.

Soon, Golden Tiger got up to gather more thatch. Golden Rabbit picked up his reaping knife to come along, but when he had taken only a few steps, he began to stagger. Thrusting one paw to his forehead as if he were faint, he said, "Some illness must be coming upon me, Friend Tiger. I must rest a little longer. I will join you as soon as I can."

Full of concern, Golden Tiger helped Rabbit settle under a tree. Then he went to the river and fetched his friend a drink of cool water. While Golden Tiger labored in the thatch field all afternoon, Golden Rabbit rested, grinning at the thought of how well his clever tricks were proceeding. By sunset, Tiger returned with a second fine bundle of thatch.

"Hallu, Friend Rabbit," Golden Tiger called as he walked across the field toward his friend. "Are you feeling better?"

But Golden Rabbit did not look better. He looked terrible. His eyes rolled up, his arms were limp, and his body shivered as if a fever were coming upon him.

"My poor friend!" Golden Tiger said in a worried voice. "I shall carry you home safely. Climb on my back and ride on the bundles of thatch. Indeed, one bundle shall be for you!" Then, with the liana vines, Tiger tied the thatch bundles across his back and Rabbit climbed weakly to the top, sprawling there in a limp heap.

Golden Rabbit felt enormously pleased with himself. *Everything is going just as I have planned,* he thought. *How Friend Tiger and I will laugh over this when we are old!*

In a short while, they reached the orchards. There, Golden Rabbit took his tinder box, struck a spark to the thatch bundles, then rolled off, shouting, "My fever! It is burning me so! I must run to the river to cool myself." In truth, however, the perfidious Rabbit ran the other way and circled through the trees.

As the worried Tiger started toward the river to see if he could help his friend, his back grew hotter and hotter. At first, he thought this was because of Rabbit's fever. But when he saw the smoke and flames, he realized he was on fire!

Tiger ran, flames streaking behind him, and plunged into the river to quench the fire. But his back was burned and blistered where the vines had fastened the burning straw closely to him.

"Poor Friend Rabbit," said Golden Tiger. "His fever is so great that it caused the thatch to burn. I must find him and help him."

Tiger looked up and down the river for his sick friend, but he could not find him. "Perhaps he has drowned!" said Tiger. And he started down the road through the woods, weeping and lamenting.

Suddenly, he saw Rabbit just ahead, calmly sitting under a camphor tree.

"Oh, Rabbit!" Tiger cried joyfully. "Are you all right?"

Rabbit pretended to be puzzled. "Good evening, Sir Tiger!" he exclaimed. "I am well, but why do you run up to me, a stranger, inquiring after my health?"

Then he paused and rubbed his chin thoughtfully. "Perhaps you have mistaken me for one of my brothers. We are many, you know."

Golden Tiger's mouth gaped in astonishment. Never before had his friend mentioned any brothers or sisters. He took a deep breath to regain his composure, apologized deeply for making such a foolish mistake, then told about how his friend, Golden Rabbit, had become very ill, so ill that he was burning with a fever.

"And...I fear my friend has drowned," concluded Tiger sorrowfully.

"Oh, that would indeed be sad," said the Rabbit, shaking

his head in deep sympathy. "But, perhaps you will find your friend farther along the river's edge. You must remember that rabbits swim very well.

"But now, look at yourself!" And with a great show of concern, Golden Rabbit inspected the blisters on Tiger's back.

"The camphor tree has excellent healing qualities," advised Rabbit. "You should rub your wounds against its bark. Then the burns will heal quickly."

Golden Rabbit felt enormously pleased with himself. *Everything is going just as I have planned. How Tiger and I will laugh over this when we are old,* he thought. And he hurried on through the trees, unnoticed by Tiger.

Tiger's blisters itched badly, and at first, rubbing them seemed to help. But the course bark tore them open and the burning and stinging soon became much worse than before. "Rabbit's brother gives bad advice!" said Tiger. The tears streamed down his face, partly from pain and partly because of worry over his poor sick friend.

Tiger had not gone far before he saw Golden Rabbit resting on the riverbank in the shade of a large boulder.

"Oh, Friend Rabbit!" Tiger called joyfully. "Are you all right?"

Again, Rabbit looked puzzled. "Good evening, Sir Tiger!" he answered. "I am well, but why do you run up asking after my health? We have never met before." Then Golden Rabbit paused and rubbed his chin thoughtfully. "Ah, perhaps you have mistaken me for one of my brothers. We are many, you know."

The Tiger hung his head for his foolish mistake and apologized. Then, once again, he told of his friend's illness.

"What a sad story!" said Rabbit. "But perhaps you will find your friend farther along the edge of the river. Rabbits swim well, you know." Then he examined Tiger's blistered, bleeding back and shook his head solemnly.

"My brother always did get confused easily," Rabbit said. "He has given you poor advice. Camphor is indeed healing, but he should not have advised you to rub yourself against the tree bark. You need something soothing, such as a plaster of cool sand or clay. Do you see the black sand on the riverbank just over there? It has exceptional healing qualities. You should roll in it. It will ease the pain."

"Am I not the cleverest of fellows?" Golden Rabbit asked himself smugly as he hurried on, unnoticed by Tiger who was busy rolling in the sand.

At first the coolness of the wet sand and mud did ease the stinging. But quickly, the sharp edges of the onyx grains cut further into the wounds, and soon Tiger's pain was greater than ever.

"This brother's advice is worse than the other's," he howled as he continued along the river's edge, weeping with pain and grief.

Just around the bend, he saw Rabbit stretched out and soaking wet on the bank of the river. Tiger gave a whoop of joy and ran eagerly, shouting, "Rabbit! Rabbit, my friend! Are you all right?" The Rabbit sat up and shook his wet fur, sending cool water drops sparkling in the sun. But, once more he pretended a look of surprise.

"Greetings, Sir Tiger. Why do you call me friend and ask if I am well? Surely we have never met. Perhaps you mistake me for one of my brothers."

Once more the poor Tiger apologized profusely for his foolish error. And once more he told the story of how his friend had become ill and run into the river. "When I saw you by the river," finished Tiger, "I had so hoped you were my dear friend, alive and well!" Then he bowed, and humbly apologized yet again.

Rabbit wiped a tear from his own face. "Sir Tiger," he said, "that is the saddest story I have heard in a long time. But do not give up hope. I know where there is a wishing well. It is not far from here. Perhaps you can find your friend through magic. Indeed, while you are there, why don't you ask to have your back healed as well. Come, I will show you."

This time, Golden Rabbit did not run on ahead, but walked in a stately manner along the path. However, he turned his head to hide the great grin he could no longer keep from his face. Soon they reached the "magic" well.

"What do you see in the well, Sir Tiger?" asked Golden Rabbit.

From where Tiger was standing, he could see only Rabbit's reflection in the water below. "Oh! My friend is in the well!" he shouted, his eyes wide with excitement.

Tiger reached down as far as he could, and suddenly, Rabbit pushed him the rest of the way. Golden Rabbit just grinned and watched the startled Tiger sink under the blue and crystal ripples, then he ran home laughing and shouting gleefully, "Rabbits swim well, Friend Tiger! How about Tigers?"

Later that evening, Golden Rabbit sat near his house still laughing. "Oh, what a clever fellow I am! How Friend Tiger and I will laugh over this when we are old!"

Just how smart is this clever Rabbit who does not seem to realize that he has probably killed his friend, Golden Tiger? Once again, mischief is not punished, but that does not overly worry the Burmese, most of whom are Buddhist. Justice, after all, will come in the next life, if not in this one, and bad deeds can be balanced by good ones. Here, perhaps Rabbit is in danger of returning as a grasshopper, a lowly worm, or even a bilu!

The Shy Quilt Bird

Like Golden Rabbit, the Naga is different in different stories. Here, he is a huge Dragon-snake, tyrant of the oceans. Everyone fears him and only the mythical Galon, a huge spirit-bird with terrible talons, can overcome him. It is one of the many paradoxes that the Tibeto-Burmans, whose customs and culture were surprisingly egalitarian, so readily accepted the Hindu concept of Divaraja (Divine King). In a way, Lion and Naga in this story reflect the two conflicting ideas of kingship which the Burmese never fully resolved.

L ion, King of all the creatures of Jambudipa, was hot and tired. "I shall go to the ocean," he decided. So he set off from his home in the high red hills.

Elephant watched him stride through the tall tawny grasses. Three small monkeys watched him saunter under the high jungle trees. Rabbit watched him step from the tangled vines and bushes that fringed the shore and walk to the water's edge.

"Ah," said Lion, "This is perfect!"

All morning, Lion played in the cool waves. He ran through the hide-and-tag ripples. He watched rainbows of fish darting through the clear water, and spied tiny snails scaling up steep rocks. Lion found prickly purple sea urchins basking in quiet tide pools, and pale blue anemones waving sinuous fingers under the rippling surge. Lion was having a wonderful time!

BUT! That very afternoon, the great Naga Dragon, King of the Sea, emerged from his dark watery home. He was tired and cold, and felt very grumpy indeed.

"Ah," he roared, "This is perfect! Now I can warm my cold

green back and my cold blue toes in this lovely hot sun." But just then, he noticed Lion sitting at the water's edge, quietly chatting with a small pink crab. The Dragon scowled at the tiny crab, who scuttled out of sight in terror. Then he glowered at Lion. But Lion only raised his eyebrows in surprise.

"Ah, King Naga. Greetings. Don't be angry. Crab is welcome here on the land. I don't mind a bit."

"Well, I mind!" snapped the Dragon. "This is my ocean! How dare you interfere with my creatures?" Then Naga Dragon stamped his feet, making rocks tremble and waves splash high.

Lion watched the Dragon's foolish tantrum. "You would be a better King if you let your people do the things that make them happy," he replied politely.

The Dragon turned purple with fury. "A King is great because he is powerful!" he bellowed. "Nobody dares disobey me! Observe!"

Nearby, three small fish leaped and chased through the sparkling waves. The Naga merely glared at them and instantly, they curled up in fright and blew away with the spindrift.

"Now! Show me your power," the Dragon demanded. "Or you shall be my supper!"

King Lion shook his head. "You are a bully, not a King. The creatures of Jambudipa know I command only when they have a dispute. They obey because they trust me to be wise and fair. That is all the power I need." Lion was right—but a bully does not like to hear the truth.

"Ha!" Naga snorted, and the toddy palms beyond the dunes shook with the mighty wind of his anger.

"You are a weakling! A prawn! A soft mango of a King! See those three small monkeys?" Naga pointed his great claw toward the edge of the jungle. "One has just tied the tails of his two companions. Destroy him for his insolence, or I shall eat you immediately!"

"Nonsense," replied Lion. "They are just playing. However, if you wish, I shall command them to stop."

King Lion opened his mouth and gave a tremendous roar. Instantly, all the sounds of the jungle ceased. Every animal froze, alert and keen, for King Lion's roar meant some terrible danger was near. Every eye turned toward the shallow churning sea, where Naga Dragon, rising from the waves, loomed over their beloved King! Every creature waited, petrified!

"See?" the Dragon chortled. "Your subjects fear me more than they fear you! Clearly I am more powerful. Therefore, fight me, or I shall eat you, NOW!"

Lion looked up at those dreadful jowls drooling above him. One snap and a gulp and.... Lion began to sweat. As a brave and mighty King, he should accept the Dragon's challenge and fight to the death. But Lion did not especially wish to become the Dragon's supper, and there could be no other end to such a fight. He needed time to think of some plan that would save both his honor and his hide.

"Great Dragon," Lion said at last, "I accept your challenge, but your strength is exceedingly great. Quite possibly I may die. Pray, grant a final favor. Allow me seven days to go to my home in the high red hills to say farewell to my family. I will return by dawn of the eighth day—King's honor!"

To Lion's surprise, the Dragon agreed. Lion slumped back through the jungle, worrying and fretting and trying to think of some clever plan. Elephant shook her head as she watched him go. But the three young monkeys scurried through the trees to find Golden Rabbit. Chattering all at once, the monkeys explained what had happened. Golden Rabbit, who was known to be clever and wise, sat back to think.

"Well," declared Golden Rabbit after some thought, "Naga Dragon won't get to eat our King if we can help it! You must find Black Mynah, the herald-bird. We shall need his help."

Off went the monkeys, leaping and swinging through the jungle. In minutes, they were back with Black Mynah at their side, and Rabbit explained his plan.

"We must ask the great Dragon-eating Galon-bird to help us. You travel all over our kingdom, so perhaps you can find him."

Black Mynah shook his head. "The Galon-bird is from the Spirit World. Even if I did find him, I do not believe he would come."

Golden Rabbit's ears flattened and his whiskers twitched. "Then, I must think again," he said finally. "Meanwhile, summon every bird and beast in all Jambudipa. Tell them what has happened. If they are willing to help, they must be here before dawn of the eighth day."

Black Mynah flew off, and Rabbit closed his eyes to think and plan.

Eight days later, in the early predawn light, Black Mynah fluttered back to the sandy strip. He hopped wearily over to greet Rabbit and pointed with one wing to the great crowd of creatures who had gathered at the jungle's edge.

"See how our brothers love King Lion?" he said proudly. "Everyone was eager to help in whatever way they could."

Rabbit nodded a greeting to them all. He was pleased to see their loyalty and courage.

Elephant spoke first. "Wise Rabbit," she said, "The Naga Dragon is not only cruel, but greedy as well. If we do not stop him, not only will he eat King Lion, but surely he will then go on to eat each of us, one by one. I suggest we all join together and charge the moment he appears. Because of my great size and strength, I would be glad to lead."

All the animals nodded eagerly. They would willingly follow Elephant and fight to save King Lion and, of course, themselves. Golden Rabbit nodded. "Your plan is good, Brave Elephant. But I believe the Naga Dragon is a bully. Often a bully can be fooled or frightened away. I think we should first try to trick him. Then, if that does not succeed, Elephant will trumpet the signal, and together we will face the Naga Dragon."

"Yes, yes," the animals agreed.

"Good," said Rabbit. "Then, let's see what we can do. We must try to make the Naga Dragon believe that one of us is the Galon-bird."

One by one, Black Mynah called the largest birds to stand before Rabbit so he could consider the possibilities. Eagle stepped forward, and Stork. Then Vulture came, and the Adjutant bird.

"Bigger—bigger!" called Rabbit shaking his head. He was beginning to fear they would have to use Elephant's plan after all.

Just then a most unusual bird stepped forward. She was almost as large as Elephant. Her feathers were a patchwork of many colors and splotches, as if great pieces of the jungle—leaves and flowers, sunlight and shadows—had all been stitched together into a giant quilt.

"My, my!" exclaimed Golden Rabbit. "I have never seen you before!" The enormous bird dropped her eyelids shyly and did not speak.

"This is the Quilt-bird," explained Black Mynah, "and she is very shy. When she stands completely still, she is extremely difficult to see, and that is how she likes it. But she wanted to do what she could for our King, so she agreed to come."

"You may be shy," said Rabbit, "but clearly you are very brave as well. Can you speak?"

The Quilt-bird nodded. "*Hou'ke* (yes)," she said in a tiny voice as soft as small sticks clattering in a breeze.

Rabbit laughed. "You could never scare the Dragon with your voice. But, never mind. I think you are just what is needed!"

Then Rabbit asked the Quilt-bird to stand partly hidden behind some trees and bushes, right by the edge of the jungle.

"Now," said Rabbit. "When Naga Dragon comes, Black Mynah will signal you with his call. Then you must flap your wings and peck at the trees and branches as though you were very angry.

"You, Leopard, must hiss. And all you monkeys must squeal as loudly as you can and hit the trees with sticks. The rest of us must hide and be very still behind the trees and bushes, for, if this first plan does not work, then Elephant will lead us against our enemy!"

Quickly everyone slipped into the shadows and shades of the jungle, just as King Lion came down the path.

All week long, Lion had thought and thought. His poor head ached from trying to think so hard. But, bravely, he had decided the only thing he could do was to come and fight the Dragon, even though it would surely be the end of him.

As Lion slumped along, Golden Rabbit hopped onto the path and sat in front of him. "Wait, Your Majesty," said Rabbit. "Please allow me to speak with the Naga before you show yourself."

"Do you think it will help?" asked Lion, holding his aching head. "The sooner the Dragon eats me, the sooner this terrible pain will stop."

"It is worth a try, Your Majesty," declared the wise Rabbit. "And if you will stand here behind these bushes, you will be able to observe how much the animals of your kingdom respect and love you."

Lion's head hurt too much to argue. Besides, he was curious to see what Rabbit and the others had planned. Just as the red-gold rays of the sun hit the crest of the waves, the sea began to churn and boil. From the splashing, dashing water, the huge Naga Dragon rose and looked all about him, but all he saw was one small rabbit sitting quietly on the sand.

"Ha!" snorted the Dragon. "I see your King is a coward! He sends a mere snippet of a Rabbit for my dinner!"

"King Lion will arrive in a few minutes," Golden Rabbit answered calmly. "He sent me ahead to tell you he was on his way." Then Golden Rabbit flicked his ears twice and Black Mynah gave his call.

A great hissing, squealing, and shrieking began. An enormous patch of jungle shivered and shook. Branches bent and trees rattled. And, above all the other noises, a terrible pecking was heard. Naga Dragon's eyes opened as wide as great white boulders. "What's that?" he cried.

"What's what?" asked Rabbit, munching calmly on a blade of grass.

"All that shaking and quaking?" whispered the Dragon. And he, too, began to shake and quake from the tip of his long blue tail to the top of his cold green nose.

"Why, I suppose that is just the Dragon-eating Galonbird," Rabbit answered. "The other day he told me he had not eaten any Dragons for nearly a month.

"Don't worry, he probably won't eat you until you have eaten Lion. By then you will be much fatter and quite delicious."

But by now, Rabbit was talking only to the wind and a swirling patch of water. As Golden Rabbit had guessed, Naga Dragon was just a bully, and often a bully can be frightened away.

The animals were so happy that they ran right over to the poor shy Quilt-bird and began to hug and kiss her for being so brave and saving them. They crowned King Lion and Golden Rabbit with wreaths of flowers, and hung garlands of golden padauk blossoms around Black Mynah's neck.

Then they danced and feasted all night and day for the next seven days. When the dancing and feasting and celebration was over, the shy Quilt-bird had been hugged and kissed so often that she was now even smaller than a sparrow. Of her great quilt coat, only a tiny patch of brown-and-white jungle shade remained. And in a tiny voice that now matched her tiny size she said, over and over, "It was nothing—it was nothing." But everyone could see how pleased she was.

Today, we call this little bird the wren. But in Myanmar she is still known as "Bird-kissed-by-the-lips." And Black Mynah proudly wears two golden wattles hanging like blossoms around his neck, to remind everyone of that great time when all the animals came together to save their King and their kingdom.

Lions were never native to Burma, but they did once roam parts of India and the countries to the west.

The Magic Mango

Cleverness, cooperation, a good Buddhist scorn toward boastfulness or excessive pride, and an awareness of nature's "clean-up crew" all figure in this tale, which is slightly reminiscent of Aesop's "The Tortoise and the Hare." In the original version, the horse merely insults the snail, and there is no mango to contest. Horse flesh itself was believed by many to have strong medicinal properties.

Snail's body ached. He had traveled a long way, and the day was near its end. Slowly he climbed up the branch of a mango tree. On the tree hung one golden mango, a Magic Mango. One bite of that mango, and Snail would never again ache or feel tired. Or so he had been told.

Just then, Horse came galloping across the rice fields, his mane flying in the wind. "Out of my way, Slow One!" Horse snorted. "I have run many miles. I am tired and must eat the Magic Mango!"

"I was here first," replied Snail politely. "I need only a small bite. Then you are welcome to eat also."

Horse snorted. "Ha! Do you expect me to eat a mango spoiled by such as you? I am Horse, the Swift One. Slow should be respectful and give way to Swift." And he tossed his head haughtily.

"Be careful, Brother Horse," Snail answered in his small quiet voice. "Perhaps I am not so slow as you believe. If you do not wish to share the Magic Mango, perhaps you will race with me, instead. Then whoever wins may eat the entire mango."

Horse whinnied in derision. "Why not?" he agreed, and

reared into the air, laughing and snorting.

"Well then," continued Snail calmly, "meet me at dawn tomorrow beside the White Pagoda, and we shall race. As I am smaller, it is my right to set the rules." Horse agreed and galloped off, still laughing. All this time, Wren had been sitting on a branch of the mango tree, watching in astonishment. Now she peered out from behind a glossy leaf and tilted her head quizzically. Snail turned toward her, grinning.

"Horse is too proud," he said. "The Swift and Great often forget that the Small and Slow share the Earth also." Little Wren nodded, remembering how Crow had snatched away her food just the day before. "Can I help?" she asked eagerly.

"Yes, indeed," replied Snail. "Go find my Cousins. Ask them to meet me by the river's edge at sunset."

Wren was puzzled, but she knew Snail was clever. "He must have a good plan," she decided, and off she flew. Before the first star sat alone in the evening sky, Snail climbed onto a large gray rock by the river. All around him crowded his Snail Cousins, all one thousand of them.

"Cousins," said Snail, "Horse believes that because he is swift he may take whatever he wants. I have challenged him to a race." Then Snail explained his plan. The Snail Cousins looked at each other and began to laugh soft, snuffling laughs.

"I see you understand!" said Snail. "Horse is so haughty that he does not look with care. He will be fooled easily."

With tiny ripples of laughter, the Snail Cousins slipped into the swift river and floated toward the White Pagoda. One by one they emerged, one Snail Cousin beside each of the furlong stones that marked the distance along the River Road. At dawn the next morning, Snail sat patiently beside the White Pagoda waiting for Horse to arrive. Most of the timid or tiny creatures of the valley had gathered to see the race, but of the great creatures, only Elephant and Crocodile had come.

"Snail is clever, but he certainly is not swift," said Lizard, shaking her head.

"He can't possibly win," agreed Butterfly.

"But, oh, wouldn't it be wonderful if he did?" whispered Mouse. Everyone nodded and continued to worry.

Elephant agreed with Mouse. She did not believe her huge size gave her, or anyone else, the right to take from the small. As for Crocodile, his only thought was how to trick someone—anyone—into becoming his dinner.

Before the sun rose over the Eastern Hills, Horse came prancing across the rice paddy. "Well, Snail," he laughed. Are you rested and ready?"

"I am ready," replied Snail. "But I must warn you that I run swiftly when I choose."

"Ha!" snorted Horse. "We shall see!"

"As to the rules," continued Snail, unperturbed, "we shall run along the River Road the thousand furlongs to the Great Mindon Bell. You are large, so I can see you easily and judge whether I am ahead. But as I am small, a stone, a lump of earth, a rut in the road may hide me from your view.

"I do not wish to slow or tire you with constantly searching about for me. Therefore, as you pass each marking stone, just call out to me and I will answer. In that manner we can both judge how we are progressing."

Crocodile, who loved neither Horse nor Snail, agreed to wait beside the great bell to judge the winner.

He slipped into the river and swam off swiftly, smiling in a manner that made all the creatures uneasy. But Snail said it would be all right. And Horse, thinking proudly how fast he was, did not worry much either.

Barking Deer was chosen to start the race. At her bark, Horse galloped off, head held high, his dark mane flying in the wind, while Snail stepped out with great dignity and walked along in a leisurely manner.

In a moment, Horse was far ahead. He slowed to a trot to save energy. At the first furlong stone, Horse felt very pleased with himself. "Well, Brother Snail, are you there?" he called. Then he whinnied and stomped his feet, laughing at his own joke.

"Here I am," a small voice answered. And there, on the road, just a few paces ahead of him, a Snail walked along sedately.

Horse was greatly astonished. How could Snail possibly be here? Assuming it was the same Snail with whom he had quarreled, and without looking closer, Horse raced off down the road with a new burst of speed.

At the next marker, Horse felt certain that by now he had left Snail far behind. But to fulfill the rules, he again called out, "Are you there, Brother Snail?"

Again a voice answered, "Here I am." Again Horse saw a Snail walking along the road just a few paces in front of him.

This made horse angry. How could Snail, who walked so leisurely, still be ahead? He snorted and ran faster still, quickly passing this Snail Cousin as well.

Each time Horse reached a marker and called out, there would be another Snail Cousin walking down the road just ahead of him. Faster and faster Horse ran, and the faster he ran, the more furious he became. The veins on his neck stood out like ropes. His body lathered from effort and fury.

Before Horse had run even half the distance to the great bell, he fell dead from exhaustion. So, of course, he never did discover Snail's secret.

Everyone cheered, and Snail was declared winner by default. That night, Snail and all his one-thousand Snail Cousins feasted together, first upon the sweet flesh of the Magic Mango, and then on the dour flesh of the Haughty Horse. And in the morning, only a pile of white bones remained gleaming in the hot sun.

Ever since the day of that great race, all snails walk about the Earth as refreshed as a child at dawn. They never feel fatigue, nor do their muscles ache, though no one knows for certain why this is so. Perhaps it is because of the magic in the wonderful Mango. Or perhaps it is because Snail, and all his Snail Cousins, continue to walk unhurried and unperturbed, and continue to help each other whenever there is a need.

And what of the Hungry Crocodile, still lurking in the river among the lotus blossoms? Well, if you are very curious, you might want to visit the great Mindon Bell yourself and find out.

The Foolish Crocodile

Once again we meet Golden Rabbit, the beloved trickster of Burmese stories. This story probably had its origin in a very similar Jataka tale in which a clever monkey fools the crocodile. However, over the centuries this story has become distinctly Burmese.

There was once a dull-witted Crocodile who lived in the muddy delta of the great Irrawaddy. One day a Rook, thinking what a delicious meal the Crocodile would make for himself and his mate, decided he would find a way to trick the great lumbering animal into becoming his dinner.

"Good morning, Friend Crocodile," said the Rook. "I have been wondering these past few days why you sit here in this shallow river, when there is a much better, deeper one only a few miles away."

"Is there?" asked the Crocodile. "I wonder why no one has ever told me of it before now?"

"Perhaps they have wanted to keep it to themselves," answered the Rook. "But I have a kind heart and will gladly show you the way."

"Is it far?" asked the Crocodile. "As you know I am heavy and slow on land and cannot travel far."

"It is scarcely more than half a mile from here," answered the Rook.

The Crocodile lumbered from the water and followed the Rook, who hopped just in front of him to lead the way. When they had traveled about half a mile the old Crocodile, panting and sweating, asked, "Is it much farther? We must have traveled a good half mile by now."

"We have gone scarcely a furlong," replied the Rook. "Surely a strong fellow like you cannot be tired."

The Crocodile was too ashamed to admit he was indeed growing tired, so he kept trudging along. After a while the Crocodile asked again, "Is it much farther?"

"We are almost there," replied the Rook, "I know the sun is hot, but think of the cool river that awaits you." So the two continued on once again.

By the time they had traveled almost three miles across the parched mud, the Crocodile collapsed from the heat. He had lost much weight from sweating and was panting from thirst. At this the Rook turned and laughed.

"Stupid creature! Now you are miles from any stream and you will soon die from heat and thirst. But be comforted. I will return in a few hours—to have you for my supper. And with that he flew away screaming his raucous laughter. The Crocodile hissed angrily at the departing Rook, then closed his eyes to accept his fate.

By good fortune, a cart man soon came down that very road. He was surprised to see the Crocodile so far from the river. The Crocodile looked up at the cart man, tears filling his eyes. "Please, good cart man," he begged, "Take me back to my river, for otherwise I will surely die."

The kindhearted carter hated to see any animal suffer, but he also knew that crocodiles were crafty animals who could not be trusted, so he took a heavy rope from his cart, bound the Crocodile's snout and feet, then hoisted him onto the cart.

When they arrived at the river, the Crocodile spoke again, his voice weak and quivering. "Good carter, I am weak and stiff from your rope. I fear I cannot even crawl from here to the water. Would you be so kind as to drive your cart into the river just deep enough for the water to reach the cart bed. That way I can slip off and float away until I regain my strength."

The carter did as the Crocodile asked, and when the water reached the height of the cart bed, the carter untied the Crocodile. He was about to wish the Crocodile good luck when the wicked animal darted to the front of the cart and grasped one of the carter's bullocks by the thigh.

"Let go of my bullock, you wicked, ungrateful animal," shouted the carter. But the Crocodile just hung on, laughing through his teeth.

Golden Rabbit happened to be sitting on the bank of the river and witnessed what had just occurred.

"Hit him with your driving stick," shouted Golden Rabbit. "Hit him hard!"

Taking the rabbit's advice, the carter thwacked the Crocodile on the snout, which smarted mightily. The Crocodile swam away, hissing and muttering that he would take revenge on Golden Rabbit next chance he got, while the carter drove away, shouting his thanks to the clever rabbit and resolving never to trust a Crocodile again, even for an instant.

Next morning, before dawn, the Crocodile swam to the river's edge. But as the river was so shallow there, the Crocodile could not entirely hide himself under the water. Instead he lay very still among the lotus leaves, pretending to be a log.

"When Golden Rabbit comes to drink, I will reward him for spoiling my dinner of fat bullock yesterday," he said, hissing a wicked laugh. Just before the sun rose over the Eastern Hills, Golden Rabbit hopped to the river to drink. The Crocodile lay very still, scarcely even breathing. But Golden Rabbit, being a wise fellow, looked carefully at the "log" caught among the reeds and lotus and called out in a loud voice: "True crocodiles swim upstream, true logs float downstream."

To prove he really was a log, the Crocodile allowed himself to float downstream for a short distance. Rabbit drank quickly and darted back into the thickets.

"Ha," thought the Crocodile, "tomorrow I won't let that rabbit fool me again." So the next morning the Crocodile again swam to the water's edge, again pretending to be a log. When Golden Rabbit came to drink, he again sang out: "True crocodiles swim upstream, true logs float downstream."

This time the Crocodile remained perfectly still, and the Rabbit, thinking this really was a log, bent down to drink. Instantly, the Crocodile snapped him into his strong jaws. But instead of gulping him right down, the Crocodile wanted to show off. He swam up and down the river with the Rabbit firmly between his teeth, thrashing about in the water and shouting, "Hee, hee, hee! Hee, hee, hee! Thee whah I caugh."

"You are a stupid fool!" Golden Rabbit called from the crocodile's jaws. "You think you are very clever. You can shout 'Hee, hee, hee,' but you are not clever enough to shout, 'ha, ha, ha!'"

The Crocodile felt insulted. Promptly he opened his mouth wide, shouting "Ha, ha, ha!" at the top of his lungs.

Golden Rabbit wasted no time at all leaping from the Crocodile's mouth, and from then on he found a safer place for his morning drink.

In one version of this story, the rabbit pulls out the Crocodile's tongue as he leaps away to freedom. He lays it near a stone and goes on his way. Soon he meets a cat, and tells her where to find the Crocodile's tongue. But when the cat arrives at the stone, she finds only a strange plant, the one called "Cat's Tongue."

Taming the Nats

It is recorded that in 442 B.C., a great earthquake shook the plain of Myingyan, thrusting skyward a great cone of volcanic ash. Over the years the ash became rich soil, and flowers covered its slopes, earning it the name Mount Popa, or flower. This strange, handsome mountain soon gained the reputation of being the special home of nat spirits.

This first semi-historical legend tells of a brother and sister, cruelly burned to death by the King of Tagaung. After their deaths, these two were believed to have been reborn as powerful spirits known as the Mahagiri Nats.

Part 1: Nga Tin De and His Beautiful Sister: The Mahagiri Nats

Near the city of Tagaung, there once lived a handsome young blacksmith and his sister. The blacksmith was so strong that his hammer could be heard ringing for miles across the land. He worked so hard that he needed to eat many bowls of rice at each meal, and he was so kindhearted that everyone loved him. Girls whispered and giggled when they saw him walking down the road, and young men were glad to call him their friend. Because his beauty was both within and without, he was called Nga Tin De, or Mr. Handsome.

Nga Tin De's beautiful sister, Shwemyethna, or Golden Face, was just as kind and helpful. Young men sought to court her, and the women of the village could always count on her to assist them in any way.

The brother and sister were so well liked that the King of Tagaung began to fear them. What if Nga Tin De wished to become King in his stead? It would be a small matter for such a popular man to gather an army of loyal friends.

Of course this was all silly nonsense. The blacksmith and his sister were well content with their lives just as they were. But the King was a fretful and suspicious man, looking everywhere for plots and enemies. The more he worried, the worse he ruled, issuing cruel punishments for any little insult he perceived, whether or not it was intended.

At last he sent a few of his elite guard to find Nga Tin De and kill him. They were to creep into his house at night and slit his throat as he slept, making it all seem as if *dacoits* had come to rob him.

One of the guards, however, was from Nga Tin De's village. He knew and admired the kindhearted blacksmith. At the risk of his own life, he managed to send word, warning Nga Tin De of the plot. Thus, when the guards reached the blacksmith's house, the young man had vanished into the forest.

About this time, the King, journeying through the village where the brother and sister lived, had seen the lovely Shwemyethna tending her garden. He was instantly smitten by her beauty and gentle manner. Inviting her to the palace, he began to woo her, and in a short time, made her one of his queens.

Little by little, the King soothed her suspicions, explaining that he had never intended to kill Nga Tin De, but only to capture him and find out for himself whether her brother had plotted to usurp the throne. Besides, he added, now that they were related, Nga Tin De would no longer be considered a rival.

Convinced of the King's sincerity, Queen Shwemyethna

sent messengers into the forest to find her brother and extend the King's invitation to join her at court.

Like many good-hearted people, Nga Tin De expected similar goodwill from others. He had no wish to live at court, but he longed to see his sister again, and to return to his smithy and his village.

Queen Shwemyethna and the King journeyed with a royal escort to the edge of the forest to welcome her brother. But as Nga Tin De emerged from the thicket, the guards seized him, bound him to a *saga* tree, piled tinder around his feet, and set him on fire.

Astonished and dismayed, Queen Shwemyethna bolted toward her brother, only to be restrained by two strong guards. At last, realizing the great perfidy of her royal husband, she cried out a curse, wrenched free of the guards, and ran to the tree, throwing herself on the flames.

Instead of ending his troubles, the King had only made things much worse for himself, for now the brother and sister had become angry Nats inhabiting the saga tree where they had met their deaths. Reports began to pour in telling of help they had given to poor villagers. And at court, terrible things began to occur. There were poxes and fevers, broken bones and lost treasures.

All over the land, the poor and oppressed began to pray to the brother and sister spirits for favors, while the powerful and dishonest trembled at the thought of the next misfortune the powerful siblings might cause.

To rid his land of these dangerous spirits, the King ordered the saga tree chopped down and thrown into the Irrawaddy.

Now, to the south, in the kingdom of Thirapyitsaya, King Thinlikyaung also heard news of these two powerful Nats.

By good fortune, he was watching beside the great river just as the saga tree floated into view. At once he called to his men to fish the tree from the water. Then he charged his best woodcarvers to make images of the brother and sister and paint them in beautiful colors.

With elaborate ceremony, the images were carried to the top of Mount Popa and placed in a shrine of their own, where, honored at last, they became benevolent, dispensing good advice, predicting the future, and offering blessings to the many pilgrims who continue to visit them to this very day.

According to *The Glass Palace Chronicles* every King from Thinlikyaung in the fourth century, to the fall of Pagan in 1287, began their rule with a pilgrimage to the shrine on Mount Popa. At this time, the brother and sister nats would make themselves visible to the new King and give him good advice.

In making the Mahagiri Nats official, King Thinlikyaung succeeded in uniting his people in a modified form of nat worship, taming somewhat the widespread animistic beliefs and incorporating them into a popular version of Buddhism.

Nevertheless, when King Anawrahta conquered the Mon kingdom in 1057, animism and nat worship were still so widespread that he and the Buddhist monks decided to endorse a roster of thirty-seven official spirits. These were then given personal histories to show that they were devout followers of the Buddha. In the centuries since, new nats have replaced old ones from time to time, but the official number has always remained thirty-seven.

Part 2: Marga, The Story of Thagya Min

There was once, in the kingdom of Yarzagyo, a young man who was called Marga. He heeded the eight-fold path of the Lord Buddha and soon became leader of a group of loyal followers, thirty-three young men who shared his ideals.

Together Marga and his friends went about the nearby villages building *zayats* and *pandalls*. They built roads and bridges, dug wells, planted and tended public gardens, assisted the old or sick, and in many other ways improved the lives of the villagers.

In turn, the villagers greatly admired Marga and his friends for their kindness and good deeds. Quarrels between neighbors were forgotten, and jealousies were set aside as one by one the villagers began to copy the shining example. The villagers, too, began to honor the teachings of the Lord Buddha, making kindness and service to others a part of their daily habit.

The Thugyi of the five villages of Marsalla, where Marga and his friends lived, was not at all pleased with the changes he saw. In the past he had received many generous bribes to settle his judgments one way rather than another. He had been given many fine gifts to cover up the illegal acts of still others, and he had profited handsomely for appointing certain men to high office. Before long, the Thugyi went to see the King.

"Sire," he said, "there is in the five villages of Marsalla a group of young men who are gathering a strong force together. They have been turning the people of these villages against you and bringing them arms and spears and elephants. My spies have been among them, and it is clear that these men will soon come to take the throne from you. I fear for your life."

King Magada was alarmed. Believing the wicked Thugyi, he immediately ordered his guards to arrest Marga and his followers and bring them to the palace where the Thugyi repeated his charges. But of course there was no trial, for who could believe the words of a traitor and would-be usurper. Instead, Marga was sentenced to death.

The guards threw Marga to the ground, while his followers, bound with strong rope, stood against the tall teak log palisade of the execution yard to witness the punishment they would share if they continued their treasonous behavior. Then a battle elephant that had been trained to kill was led into the enclosure.

Safely seated in a watchtower high above the enclosure, the King lifted his hand to signal that the execution should commence, but just as the elephant lifted his great foot, Marga called out, begging to speak a farewell to his friends. The King nodded, the elephant was backed away, and Marga spoke as follows: "Friends, forgive the Thugyi for his distortions. He is the captive of jealousy. Bear him no grudge, but only continue to offer love. Remember the eight-fold path we have followed together. Honor the King, for he has been deceived. Respect the elephant, for he only acts as he has been taught. Above all else, fail not to love."

With that, the elephant was ordered forward.

Marga's friends stood by bravely, showing no hatred and no fear, their faces glowing with the command to love. Over and over the elephant raised his foot to crush the young leader, but feeling the aura and power of love from Marga and all the young men, the elephant was unable to bring his foot down on the holy youth. After many attempts, he trumpeted loudly, broke his bonds and tore away into the jungles.

The astonished King turned to Marga and asked what magic sayings he had to prevent the elephant from following the *oozie's* command.

"Sire," replied Marga, "I have no magic. I have only the Lord Buddha's precepts, which I follow with diligence."

King Magada was so impressed by what he had just seen and the quiet words of this pious youth that he immediately released him and all his followers. The King also gave Marga all the possessions of the greedy Thugyi and sentenced him to serve the youth for the rest of his days.

In the following years, Marga and his friends doubled their efforts, traveling far and wide, teaching by their example, sharing and helping others. By the time of their deaths, Marga and his friends had acquired so much merit that they were reborn in *Tawadaintha Nat Pyi* (Blessed Land of the Nats). Marga became their King and was known as the *Thagya Min,* and he and his followers became the "good-willed *nats.*"

Part V: Jataka Tales

The World's Oldest Stories

The Jataka tales are some of the world's oldest stories. They were brought from India along with Buddhism, and belong to the Burmese in much the same way that fairy tales from Europe and Bible stories from the Near East belong to American children.

By Buddhist tradition, the Jatakas are tales of the Buddha's previous lives, and show how he gradually accumulated wisdom and moral insight. But the truth is, most of these stories originated long before the Buddha lived and taught. There is also reason to believe that Aesop's famous fables may have roots in these same Indian stories. Like Aesop's stories, most Jatakas have a moral lesson. Others are "just for fun," and a few "explain" how things were long ago.

Centuries ago, many of these tales were illustrated in colored clays on ceramic tiles and placed in pagodas, where they can still be seen today. These picture tiles served as a "Poor Man's Bible" for the multitude who were unable to read. Often a single picture could bring to mind an entire story, for everyone would have heard these tales time and time again sitting at the feet of their *pongyi* teachers—and on those magical nights when the old Storyteller would arrive to begin recounting the myths, legends and fables treasured by all the people of Burma.

The Pious Jackal

A scoundrel hiding behind a holy disguise must be as old as religion itself. The remarkable thing is this ancient Jataka story warning the young to beware.

In a great jungle there once lived a Rat King and all his subjects. They were so numerous they consumed all the rice from the fields for miles around. To keep from starving, some rats would leave from time to time to find homes in distant jungles.

One day a crafty Jackal arrived in the Rat King's jungle. Now, rats were his favorite food, and seeing so many rats he sat down to think of a plan.

"Ah, I have it," he thought. Whereupon he stood up on one hind leg, opened his mouth, and pointed his head toward the sky. That evening as usual, the rats went out into the fields to find rice and other seeds. A curious young Rat noticed the Jackal standing in this odd posture.

"Why do you suppose that Jackal stands in so unusual a pose?" he asked a fellow Rat. Soon all the rats were staring at the Jackal and whispering among themselves.

"Perhaps he is keeping some religious vow," guessed one old Rat. The first Rat went up to the Jackal. He cleared his throat. "Excuse me, Sir Jackal," said the young Rat. "What is your name, please."

The Jackal, moving only his mouth answered, "I am called Dhannaka." And so saying he again opened his mouth and resumed his strange position.

"Excuse me again, Sir Jackal," continued the curious Rat.

"But why do you stand on one leg?"

"Ah, Young Seeker of Answers, it is because of the weight of my thoughts. If I were to stand on all four legs, my weight could very well crush the earth."

The listening rats whispered excitedly. "Such a wise Jackal," said some. "Such a holy creature," said others.

Again, the curious young Rat went up to the Jackal. "Sir Jackal, please explain why you stand with your mouth open."

"Ah, Young Seeker of Understanding, it is because I feed only on air."

At this, the wide-eyed rats again murmured among themselves, deeply moved by the Jackal's answer.

Once more the young Rat inquired, "Sir Jackal. Tell us why your head looks constantly to the sky?"

"Ah, Young Seeker of Wisdom," the Jackal replied, "it is because the Sun is the Giver of Blessings to the Earth. I worship him and praise his greatness." And, maintaining his strange pose, the Jackal began a sermon on the lessons that the clouds impart.

The rats, immensely impressed, began coming each morning and evening to hear the Jackal expound on wondrous things. At the end of each sermon, the rats marched off in a solemn procession. However, just as the last Rat started around the bend in the path, the Jackal would pounce, gulp his victim before it could cry out, then quickly wipe his mouth and resume his pious pretense.

This continued for some months, for the rats were not especially quick-witted. But one day the young, curious Rat said to his companion, "Does it not seem to you that there are fewer and fewer of us of late?"

"Why, yes," the other Rat answered, a little surprised. "I

did notice that now the rice grows faster than we eat it and that the ponds hold sufficient water for all."

"Perhaps we should speak to the King," said the first Rat.

So the two went to find the King. "Your Majesty," said the young, curious Rat. "Does it not seem to you that our numbers are becoming smaller?"

The old King nodded, for he was somewhat brighter than many of his subjects. "Yes, my fine young man," he said. "I have begun to notice just that of late. I have had difficulty recruiting soldiers or builders or farmers. Furthermore, we have not sent settlers to other jungles for quite some time. I will come at once to investigate."

To himself, the King muttered, "I suspect that Jackal has something to do with this. I believe he is neither holy nor honest."

When the King reached the place where the pious Jackal preached each day, he called together a large number of rats. "Tonight," he said, "I will go with you to hear the Jackal, but when it is time to leave, you must allow me to go last."

"Oh, no, Your Majesty," protested the rats. "That would not be honorable."

"Is it not your prime duty to obey me?" questioned the King. The rats agreed that it was. "Then do as I bid," he commanded.

That evening, after the sermon, the King remained behind the others and started down the path last of all. As soon as most of the procession was out of sight, the Jackal dropped to all four feet and sprang at the Rat King. But the King was ready. Turning swiftly, he leaped at the Jackal's throat, gripping it firmly with his sharp teeth. Then, through his clenched jaw, the Rat King muttered, "You wicked creature, your pious pretense will deceive us no longer. You have had your last meal."

With that, the Rat King bit deeply until the Jackal lay dead. And that night, it was the rats who ate Jackal for their dinner!

The Crab and the Crane

In both this and the previous tale, the listener is reminded that the leopard is unlikely to change his spots, the jackal his hunting nature, or the crane his habit of eating fish.

There was once, in the deep jungle, a pond that was home to many fine silver fish. Throughout the months of rain, the fish had plenty of water. They would swim and play and nibble lily roots and duckweed until they grew fat and delicious. But when the months grew hot and dry, the water evaporated and the pond would shrink. Then the fish would gasp for breath and grow thin for lack of food.

One day a Crane, stopping by this pond, saw the many fat fish. His mouth watered as he watched them swimming about. "I could stand in the shallow water and stalk my supper," he said to himself, "but that is too much work. Fish are stupid. Perhaps I can trick them instead." And that night he thought of a plan.

The next morning, the Crane stood on one leg among the reeds and pretended to be deep in thought. After a while, one curious Fish, keeping a safe distance away, asked, "What are you thinking about, Uncle Crane?"

"I was begging the Buddha to be merciful to you now that the hot months have begun and your pool is beginning to shrink. Perhaps he will show me a way to assist you."

Greatly impressed, the young Fish reported what he had said. An old Crab, listening, shook his head. "It is a trap. Since the world began, no Crane has ever had any thought for a fish except to plan how best to catch and eat it." And the old Crab crawled away.

"But maybe this Crane is different," replied the young Fish, and he swam back to talk with the Crane. A wise old Fish went with him.

"This young Fish tells us that you are trying to think of a way to make our life more pleasant in the hot months ahead," said the old Fish.

"Yes, yes," replied the Crane. "Indeed, I have found a way. A few miles from here is a much larger lake filled with lotus, and fed by a mountain stream which keeps it full all year 'round. Lord Buddha has led me to it and I have just now returned. If you will allow me, I will gladly carry you, one by one, to the new pond."

The old Crab, who had crept along the shore to where the Crane stood, again shook his head. "Don't believe him," he grumbled.

By now, a number of Fish had gathered to hear the Crane. Their eyes widened at the thought of the pleasant lake, always full of cool fresh water and plenty of lotus leaves for shade and food. "If just one of you will trust me, I will show you that what I say is true," the Crane said.

Knowing that his life must be near its end anyway, the old wise Fish offered to go with the Crane. "This shall be my last and best service to my fish brothers," he thought to himself. "Perhaps it will gain me merit."

Turning to his fellow fish, he said, "If I do not return, my friends, you will know the Crane is lying. Remember me with kindness." And with that he allowed the Crane to pick him up with his sharp beak.

Before long they reached a fine lake, just as the Crane had promised. "Swim here a while, old fellow," the Crane said in a soothing voice. "See whether I have not spoken truly." And he released the old Fish, who swam through the cool currents of the mountain stream, and between the stalks of numerous lotus stems and water grasses.

Soon, the old Fish returned to the Crane. "Take me back to my pond," he urged, "for you surely do not exaggerate. This lake is as wonderful as you report. And you must pardon me for doubting you."

"Tut, tut, old fellow," the Crane replied. "Think nothing of it."

The Crane carried the old Fish back to his own pond where he told all the other fish the wonders of the lake. "And as you can see, the Crane has returned me safely. What a good and unusual fellow he is!"

"Good, good. It is settled, then," said the Crane. "Who will be first?"

The old Fish requested the honor. Once again, the Crane picked him up carefully and flew off toward the lake. But just before they reached its shore, the Crane began to fly in a new direction.

"Say, old fellow," said the surprised Fish, "surely this is not the way."

"Ha!" laughed the Crane. "Did you really think I wished to help you? You are just a stupid Fish and good for nothing but a fine meal." With that, the Crane settled in a thorn tree near the lake, devoured the Fish and threw his bones on the ground below. Then he flew back to the pond.

"Who will be next?" asked the Crane. One by one, he carried each eager fish to the thorn tree. Soon the ground beneath the tree was littered with fish bones, and no one remained in the pond but the old Crab and a family of turtles.

"Who will be next?" asked the Crane, flying back one more time.

The old Crab crawled along, grumbling. "No fish remain in this pond, Mr. Crane," he said, "And I still do not believe you."

"Come with me, and I will show you how happy your friends are. I am certain they would rejoice in your company," replied the deceitful fellow.

"But your beak, like my shell, is hard and smooth," objected the Crab. "I might slip and fall to my death. If I may grasp the feathers of your neck with my strong claw I would not slip."

Thinking that the Crab was too stupid to plan a trick, the Crane agreed. The Crab took a firm hold around the Crane's neck and off they flew. Soon, the Crab could see the sparkling lake below and began to think that he had misjudged the bird. But just as they neared the shore, the Crane veered toward the thorn tree with its great pile of Fish bones.

"Oh, you are indeed a wicked thing," cried the Crab. "Not only have you eaten all of my friends, but you tricked them with your lies. But you shall not eat me, for if you try, I shall pinch off your head and we shall fall to our deaths together." Then he tightened his claw around the Crane's neck until the bird gasped for breath and tears flowed from his eyes.

"Spare me, wise Mr. Crab—good Mr. Crab," the tearful Crane pleaded, "I never intended to eat a clever fellow like you. You are not like the stupid Fish, who should have known they are my natural dinner."

"Then return me to my pond," demanded the old Crab.

The Crane obeyed, and they soon landed safely by the edge of the water. But instead of dropping into the mud, the Crab promptly snipped off the Crane's head and scurried into his old burrow.

Thus, the Crane paid the penalty for his treachery and lies.

How Turtle Saved His Life

This Jataka tale has much in common with the story of "Tar Baby," where the rabbit pleads: "Don't throw me in the briar patch. Please! Anything but that!"

There was once a King who had four little sons of whom he was very fond. For their pleasure he ordered his gardeners to build a large pond in the palace gardens, siphoning the needed water from a nearby stream, which happened to flow on into a great river.

The four young princes were delighted with their new pond. They splashed and swam and sailed their small boats. They picked lilies, and ran to show the star-like blossoms to their father.

One day the King told his little sons that the gardener had brought some fish to the pond for them to enjoy. They loved to see the fish and feed them pieces of bread. Excitedly, they pointed out the different shapes and colors, until one young prince noticed a strange animal sitting on the mud bank beside the pond.

This animal was none other than an old brown Turtle who lived in a nearby stream, which happened to flow down a steep rocky slope and on into the great river beyond. But the four princes, having never seen a such a creature before, ran screaming to their father that a water demon had come to their pond.

The King listened to the frightened boys and ordered the head gardener to bring this demon at once. When the King saw what the "demon" was he smiled, but because the little boys were still frightened, he asked them what they wished him to do with this demon.

"Kill it, Kill it!" the boys shouted at once. So the King ordered the gardener to take the demon away and kill it.

When the head gardener returned to the pond, he told the other gardeners the King's command. "But what is the best way to kill a Turtle?" he asked the others.

"Throw it in boiling water," said one.

"Crush it with a rock and bury it," said another.

But the third gardener, who was mortally afraid of water said, "Throw it into the stream where the water spills over the rocks. If the fall does not kill it, it will surely drown in the swift flowing river below. Either way that would certainly be the end of it."

At these words, the Turtle poked his head out and called loudly, "Mercy, mercy, good people! What have I done to deserve such a cruel death? Your other plans were bad enough, but spare me this most horrible of fates."

At once the head gardener ordered the Turtle thrown into the spillway where the pond water flowed back down into the river. As the Turtle tumbled through the splashing water, he remained motionless, pretending to be dead. But when he reached the river, he swam away happily, rejoicing that the King's gardeners did not know they had returned him to his home.

Harsh Words

As with most of the Jataka tales, the location of this story remains in northern India, while other Jataka tales were given new settings in Myanmar (or Burma, as it was known for centuries). For example, the story of "The Foolish Crocodile" is set in the Irrawaddy delta, and the stories of Wise Rabbit in "The Case of the Calf and the Colt," of Learned Princess in "Rope of Pearls," and of King and kingdom in "The Measure of Rice," have become thoroughly Burman.

Once, in the northern kingdom of Gandhara, a fine bull calf was presented to a noble Brahmin as a gift. The Brahmin was so pleased, he named the animal Great Joy. He personally fed the calf on the best rice meal, and allowed the calf to run and play freely in a grassy pasture. The Brahmin tended him morning and night, brushing his amber coat and telling him what a fine animal he was.

With such kindness, Great Joy thrived and in time became a huge beast of extraordinary strength. "I am the strongest bull in all India," he said to himself, "though probably no one knows it but myself. My master does not require me to labor for my care nor does he display me in the town." And with that, Great Joy tried to think of some way to repay the Brahmin for all his kindness.

One morning Great Joy went to his master and said, "Sir, if you can, find some rich man and wager a thousand pieces of gold that no bull of his can match my strength.

The surprised Brahmin looked at the rippling muscles of Great Joy and stroked his massive shoulders. "Are you certain?"

asked the Brahmin, for his entire wealth barely exceeded the amount of the wager.

"Yes, I am certain," replied the bull. "I can draw a load of one hundred carts filled with stone."

The delighted Brahmin went into the town. There he found a rich merchant who laughed at the Brahmin's boast.

"One hundred loaded carts?" the merchant exclaimed with a smirk. "My oxen are among the strongest to be found anywhere," he said, "but the best among them cannot pull more than fifty loaded carts. Are you certain you wish to part with so much of your gold?"

The Brahmin said he was sure, and the wager was arranged for the next morning. Nervously, the Brahmin wandered about the market observing the carters driving their oxen with shouts and curses, often lashing them with the whip. Although the beasts looked miserable and unhappy, they nevertheless strained and pulled the heavy loads.

When the next morning arrived, the Brahmin and Great Joy arrived at the market. There, the hundred carts were loaded with stone and sand. The Brahmin gave Great Joy a good meal of rice, then he climbed into the driver's seat himself, raised his whip and snapped it loudly in the air.

"Now you great dumb beast, pull!" the Brahmin cried.

The startled animal had never heard the Brahmin speak this way before, and stood where he was.

"Pull, you stupid thing, you wicked devil. Pull, I say," shouted the Brahmin, becoming still more nervous.

The bull could hardly believe his ears. *Devil? Stupid? Dumb? I am none of these things! Why is my friend and master insulting me so, and within the hearing of all these people?* And with that thought, the bull stubbornly planted his feet four square on the road and would not budge.

The frustrated Brahmin at last unharnessed his bull, paid the merchant, and hurried back to his house with the jeers and laughter of the townspeople ringing in his ears. He flung himself on his bed in agony, though the sun still shone.

Great Joy, still puzzled by his friend's behavior, made his way slowly towards the fields where he usually grazed. Passing by the Brahmin's window, he looked in. "Are you taking a nap, Sir?" asked the bull.

"A nap!" shouted the Brahmin. "I shall probably never sleep again. Did you hear the people jeering? And most of my gold is gone. Why did you not pull the load as you promised?"

"Why did you insult and shame me before all those people?" replied Great Joy. "Do I not have feelings as well? I am not 'stupid' nor 'a devil,' as you called me. Have I ever crashed through your home breaking things as some bulls do? Have I ever trampled your garden, or frightened your children, or left my soil in your path? Until today you have treated me with great kindness. Were you so greedy for the merchant's gold that you forgot to treat me with respect?"

For some minutes the Brahmin sat silently, overcome with shame.

"You are right, old friend," he said at last. "In my fear, I copied the actions of the village carters when they wish their oxen to pull heavy loads."

"And do their oxen look fit or content?" replied Great Joy. "I assure you I can pull the one hundred loaded carts. Go again to the merchant, and this time wager two thousand gold pieces. He will be more than glad to take your bet. But this time, do not belittle or insult me."

As Great Joy predicted, the merchant listened with

amusement to this strange Brahmin, who was so willing to part with his wealth. Gladly he accepted this second wager.

When the carts were loaded once more, the Brahmin climbed on to the drivers seat. He merely waved his driving stick cheerfully and called out, "Now, my good bull, let's show everyone what a strong, fine fellow you are. Ready? Pull then, my Great Joy, pull!"

With a single heave of his tremendous shoulders, the bull moved forward, the loaded carts creaking along behind until the last cart stood where the first had been.

The happy Brahmin collected the two thousand gold pieces amid the cheers of the crowd, and for years afterward, people spoke of the great bull and his amazing strength.

As for the Brahmin, he never again forgot to treat others with kindness and respect.

The Travelers' Tales

These four short Jataka tales are separate stories and are not traditionally grouped together. The travelers have been added to provide a setting and a human voice to state each "lesson."

One night, four travelers all stopped at the same rest house. After they had cooked their meal, they sat about watching the moon through the jungle trees.

"Let us tell some stories," said the first traveler. So it was agreed, and the first traveler began his tale:

"There was once a blind man who set off to the bazaar on a dark, moonless night. On his head he balanced a jar filled with good rich honey, which he steadied with one hand. In his other hand he carried a lantern.

When he reached the bazaar, a young fish merchant who was setting up his stall jeered, saying 'You must be stupid as well as blind, you foolish fellow. Night and day are the same to you, yet you burden yourself with a lantern and waste the cost of its oil.'

The blind man laughed good-naturedly. 'The lantern is not for me,' he said. 'It is for you. Without it, you might have crashed into me and broken my jar of honey.'

So the fish merchant set about, minding his own business, both humbler and wiser than before."

"And so it is with learning," said the first traveler. "The light of knowledge enriches teacher and pupil alike."

The others nodded in agreement, then the second traveler began:
"There was once a group of merchants who agreed to

travel together from village to village. At each village they would set up their wares for a day or two and then travel on. Dacoits were less likely to attack a caravan, and the merchants' mutual fellowship was welcome on the long journeys.

One month, in the hot, dry season, their route crossed a long stretch of sandy wasteland. For two days they traveled, and still they were in the desert. Four days more they journeyed, but no lake or stream or even a tiny spring could be found. By now all their water jars were empty as well.

That night, the merchants were faint and miserable. 'We shall die, we shall die,' they moaned.

But one merchant walked far to each side of the road, still searching for some source of water. As he sat on a rock to rest, he noticed one small bush which looked fresh and green although for miles around other plants were shriveled and brown.

'If this bush is green, there must be water,' decided the merchant.

At once he went to the camp where the others had fallen into a fitful sleep. 'Wake, you sleepy fellows, and come with me. I have found green plants. There must be water nearby.'

The others got up and went with the persistent merchant. 'I don't see any water,' said one and the others agreed.

'For this plant to be so prosperous,' he told his fellow merchants, 'the water must be within reach of its root. If we dig we may find its source.'

But the other merchants shook their heads, saying they were tired and week and did not wish to dig.

'Is it better to dig, or better to die?' asked the first merchant.

Reluctantly, the others agreed it was better to dig, so they went to their ox carts, got out their shovels and hoes, and came back to dig, grumbling all the while.

Soon they could hear the gurgling sound of water. Everyone cheered and began to dig faster and more willingly, but their shovels soon struck a rock of great size. They dug to this side and that, but the rock stretched in every direction, and although the roots of the bush pierced a narrow crack, the merchants could not break the rock.

'It is our karma to die here,' they agreed. 'We may as well sleep and forget our discomfort.' So they went back to lie down on their mats beside their carts.

All but the one stubborn merchant.

All night, he chipped and chopped at the rock, hammering near the tiny cracks through which the plant's roots had found their way. Little by little, the crack grew larger until at last the rock was broken through and the hole filled with sweet water.

How the others rejoiced the next morning to find their lives had been spared. They and their oxen all drank their fill, reflecting on the wisdom of diligence and its power to improve one's karma."

"Yes," agreed the third traveler, "the Lord Buddha Himself often spoke of the courage to persist." And thus he began the third tale:

'It is said that at one time the Lord Buddha came to rest beside a lake in the forest. He was weary and discouraged, for he had spent many years in searching and meditating. He had listened to the wisdom of many sages and soothsayers, but none could tell him why the earth was filled with sorrow and cruelty, pain and greed.

Perhaps there is no answer, he thought. *Perhaps it is useless to search.*

Just then, he noticed a small red squirrel behaving in a most unusual manner.

The squirrel would run to the lake, dip his tail into the water, then return a short distance and shake his tail vigorously over the dry land.

'What are you doing?' the Lord Buddha asked.

'I am emptying this lake,' answered the squirrel. The gentle Prince smiled and held the squirrel in his hand. 'Little Friend,' he said. 'Go back to your nest and play with your friends. Not even if you lived a thousand years, and spent all your days dipping water, would you be able to empty that great lake.'

'Are you certain?' asked the squirrel.

'Yes, quite certain,' answered the Lord Buddha.

The squirrel paused a moment to consider. He looked at the kindly face, then at the lake. 'Well, I am not discouraged,' he said at last. 'If I persist, I will at least approach my goal. In any case, I simply must try,' and with that the squirrel ran back to the water's edge and continued his dipping.

'You are indeed wise, Little Squirrel,' the Lord Buddha said to himself. 'It is your karma to instruct me, for even though I never succeed, I, too, simply must try.'"

The travelers nodded together over the squirrel's wisdom. Then turning to the fourth traveler, they said, "Now tell us your tale."

"My tale is of three friends—a Crow, a Stag and a Tortoise who lived near a certain lake. One day a passing hunter saw the hoof marks of the Stag. *Aha*, thought the hunter, *this is a fine large Stag. It will provide many meals for my family as well as a valuable pelt to sell.* So he set his net and a trap to spring it, and went on his way.

That evening, when the Stag came from his forest glade to drink and visit with his friends, his hoof touched the trigger. Instantly the net fell over him, trapping him in its web. His friend, the Crow, waited by the lake as usual, but of course the Stag did not appear. After a while, Crow flew to a high branch and soon noticed the Stag caught in the hunter's net.

At once Crow flew to the edge of the lake and called to Turtle. 'Stag has been caught in a hunter's net,' he said, 'How can we help him?'

'Be calm,' said Turtle. 'I shall bite through the net cord and free him.'

'I shall help too,' said Crow. 'I can bring water in my beak to soften the cord.'

The two worked all night while Stag waited hopefully, but by dawn the cord was only half bitten through.

'I fear the hunter will come soon,' said Crow. 'I shall fly into that high tree and warn you when he approaches.'

Soon, Crow saw the hunter coming down the path, and cawed his warning. The Stag bucked in terror, pulling and tossing his great antlers. By good fortune, his great strength and panic snapped the last threads of the net and Stag ran swiftly into the forest, with the hunter in pursuit.

When it was clear that he could not catch the Stag, the hunter returned for his net. Spying the large Turtle making his way slowly back to the lake, the hunter said to himself, 'A small meal is better than none.' Whereupon he grabbed the animal by one leg and thrust it into his game bag.

Crow saw all this and flew rapidly into the forest, calling to Stag.

'Stag, Stag. Our friend Turtle is now caught in the hunter's bag. If you will cross the hunter's path pretending that you are lame, I believe the hunter will put down his bag and follow you again. I will fly along and tell you what happens.'

Stag did as Crow suggested.

When the hunter saw the great animal limping along just a short way ahead, he thought, 'Aha! So you wounded yourself, did you? You won't escape me this time.' Then he hung his game bag on a low branch and gave chase.

Crow flew overhead cawing, but of course the hunter could not understand his words. 'Lead the hunter in a round-about path,' Crow told Stag. 'His bag hangs from a low tree branch. You will be able to circle back and release it.'

Stag limped just ahead of the hunter until they had gone some distance, then in a burst of speed he circled back to the tree, lifted the bag from the branch with his antler, and released Turtle. And the three hurried off in a different direction, rejoicing in each other's company.

Thus, even though earth may be full of pain and sorrow, cruelty, and injustice, love is wiser and stronger than all these."

With that the four travelers blew out their lamps and slept in peace.

Chronology of Burmese History

500 B.C.	Gautama Buddha (623-544) lives and preaches in India.
480	Shwe Dagon Pagoda founded (by Mon) as a small stupa over sacred Buddha relics.
442	Mt. Popa, a volcanic core, is extruded during an earthquake.
3rd century	Suvannabhumi (The Golden Land) is established at Thaton by Mon-Khmer people. Literate and cultured, they keep strong ties to Sri Lanka and India. Legend says King Ashoka of India sent monks to Thaton and other coastal areas of Southeast Asia, establishing Theravada Buddhism throughout the region.
1st century A.D.	Pyu, Tibeto-Burman people arrive, build Sri Ksetra ("City of Splendor") during first century near modern Prome. Records are poor, mostly of oral tradition. However, Chinese records from third century A.D. also mention the Pyu.
108	Pagan first settled by Pyu according to tradition. First verifiable date for Pagan is A.D. 832.
4th century	Arakan, kin to Pyus and Burmans, establish several states on western coast. Strong trade and Buddhist ties with India. Considerable intermarriage.
8th century	Pyu move their capitol north along the Irrawaddy to Halin. Han, a Thai people from Yunnan, migrate into eastern mountains and upper plain of Irrawaddy/ Chindwin, and conquer, enslave, or disperse the Pyu.
9th century	Burman (Mramma) people migrate into "Upper Burma" establishing their capital at Pagan, bringing Tantric Ari Buddhist monks and ingrained animistic beliefs. Burmese legend includes the former Pyu Kings as part of the Burman royal line.
1057	First Burmese Empire; Anawrahta Min, first general to use elephants in war, conquers the Mon capital, Thaton, brings their king, their culture and Theravada Buddhism to Pagan. In his devotion to this new, much less super-

stitious Buddhism, he ousts the Ari Monks and denounces their teachings. The Burmese alphabet is created about this time in order to translate and transcribe the Pali scriptures into the Burmese language.

1084–1167   Pagan's "Golden Age" blossoms with Kyanzittha and Alaungsithu. By 1257, Pagan is widely known as the "City of Four Million Pagodas." Kublai Kahn sends Marco Polo as envoy to see and report. The Kahn, deeply religious, wishes to learn more of Pagan's beliefs and customs. He tries to negotiate ties. But the vain and stupid Narathipate Min considers the Mongols unimportant, and insults the envoys.

1287   Kublai Kahn and the Mongols conquer Pagan. First Burmese Empire ends. During the next 300 years Burmese kingdoms are fractured, and power shifts mostly between the Shan and the Mon with a long period of wars. The Shan move into the power gap left by the Mongols. They soon control central Burma, making their capital first at Sagaing, later at Ava (both near modern Mandalay), and subjugating many Burmans. Others flee, many to Toungoo. The Mon use this period to establish the Talaing Empire at Martaban, later moving it north to Hamsawaddy, "Duck River," now Pegu, in 1369. Pegu becomes a center of religious study and reform under Binnya U, beginning a new golden age of Mon culture.

1453–1492   Dhammazedi and Queen Shinsawbu, beloved Mon rulers, continue the reforms. Meanwhile, European explorers begin to arrive and negotiate for trading rights.

15th century   De Brito, a Portuguese trader, "crowns" himself king of Syriam in 1600, but is executed thirteen years later.

1541   Second Burmese Empire. Tabinshweti Min founds the Toungoo Dynasty. After conquering Mon Pegu in 1539, he seizes Prome from the Shan, once more uniting upper and lower Burma. In 1555 his brother, Bayinnaung, recaptures Ava and tries to extend Burmese

	borders into Siam and Arakan. But Burman power wanes with new Shan and Arakanese victories.
1755	Third Burmese Empire. Alongpaya Min begins the Konbaung Dynasty. He unifies the Burmese, retakes Ava from the Mons, founds Yangon (Rangoon)—meaning "End of Strife" and carries his campaign into Siam (Thailand). But the Siamese king refuses to acknowledge him as the future Buddha, so he lays siege to the capitol, but dies of a fever before his campaign succeeds. His son, Hsinbyushin Min, continues the aggression, killing the king of Siam in the process. This act refuels the longstanding enmity between the two kingdoms.
1782–1819	Bodawpaya Min, Alongpaya's fourth son, believes he is the Buddha reincarnated. Ruthless, he begins raids on Burmese rebels and British garrisons in Arakan. His grandson Bagyidaw succeeds him, continuing the raids.
1824–1826	First Anglo-British War. Arakan and Tenasserim become British protectorates. Bagyidaw and his successors are vain, corrupt, and ineffective. The British intervene in a dispute between two British merchants. It is mostly a convenient excuse to expand the British Empire.
1852–1853	Second Anglo-British War gives the British control of all Lower Burma.
1853–1878	Mindon Min, interested in peace and in understanding Western technology, deals surprisingly well with the British. In 1861, he moves his capital to Mandalay, but Westerners watch, horrified, at the traditional custom of providing ghost guardians by burying people alive under palace walls and gate posts. In 1871, Mindon gathers the Fifth Buddhist Synod in Mandalay, has the Tripitaka recorded on tablets and enshrines them at Mandalay Hill. Thibaw, manipulated by his wife, Supayalat, becomes king. The British now watch a new menu of heinous murders, including the massacre of the rival princes by the Royal War Elephants. Again, Thibaw's Buddhist concept of the cosmos contributes to his

	misjudging and insulting, the British. His worst mistake is to seek an alliance with the French. Thibaw's cruelty gives the British an excuse to declare war.
1885	Third Anglo-British war. Thibaw is defeated and exiled. Britain takes over all of Burma, ruling it as a province of British India.
1930	The thirty Thakins lead the student push for reform in the schools and for freeing Burma from its British yoke. While these goals united the Thakins, their visions for the future are not the same. The Thakins, led by Aung San, turn to Japan for help in ousting the British, unaware it will be a costly bargain. The Japanese quickly become the new, cruel masters. Under Aung San the Thakins realign themselves with Britain, first obtaining promises that independence would follow the hoped-for victory.
1948	Independence from Britain, and a period of new hope.
1962	Ne Win's military coup begins a period of cruel dictatorship. His proclaimed goal is to unite the warring factions of Burma, exclude all non-Burmese, and establish Burmese Buddhist Socialism as he envisions it. Instead, the highly corrupt Ne Win regime has raped the land of its considerable natural wealth.
1988	National League for Democracy is created by Bo Aung Gyi and Daw Aung San Suu Kyi, daughter of Aung San. Daw Suu Kyi (Sue Chee) wins the permitted election, but the military junta negates the result, placing Suu Kyi under house arrest.
1991	Suu Kyi, still confined, is awarded the Nobel Peace Prize for her courage to speak.

At the end of the twentieth century, Burma struggles to achieve democracy and unity—moving toward twenty-first century possibilties.

Glossary

Ah-ma-le!	"Oh Mother!" Exclamation used in distress. Also *A-ma-le!*
aingyi	A woman's blouse, waist length, often sheer. Also *eingyi*. Worn over a white cotton bodice trimmed with lace.
Alompraw	(Properly, *Alaung Payar*, "Sacred Body"). A Burmese king who ruled during the latter half of the eighteenth century.
betel	Leaf of a pepper tree chewed with lime; results in a red slurry.
betel-box	Box, often of lacquerware, containing the kit for chewing betel (lime, pepperleaf, scissors, etc.) Betel produces a mild euphoria. It also turns the chewer's saliva red and rots the teeth.
Boddhisatva	Emerging Buddha, who loses individual consciousness to become one with the universal essence.
Boh (Bo)	Chief, Leader, especially a military leader or bandit chief. (literally "Lord").
bombees*	Baggy trousers characteristic of Indian attire.
chinthe	Mythical winged lion-dog. Statues of these creatures frequently guard pagodas.
chattee*	Clay vessel for rice, water, etc., often large enough to hold a person.
cheroot*	Long cigar (see *salay*).
chinlon	A wicker ball, used in a favorite game. Players form a circle and try to keep the ball in the air using only feet and knees.
dacoit	Thief, bandit.
dah	Knife, sword—any sharp blade.
dahmah	Kitchen knife.

*Indian word

224

Daw	A title of respect for an older woman (literally "Auntie").
dhobi*	Washerman.
downjah*	Wooden sleeping platform.
gaungbaung	Man's head scarf of brightly colored silk wound over a closely fitting wicker frame and tied with a jaunty "ear" at the side.
gon-bin	Mischief-maker tree. Also ohn-bin (see *ohn*).
hintha	Mythical bird, favored steed of one of the nats; also symbol of the Mon Royal family.
hnget pyaw bu	Banana bud, a shape often used in pagodas.
hpya	A mat, used ubiquitously for sitting, eating, and sleeping; rolled and carried on journeys.
htaminok	Rice container, used for serving rice and other foods.
hte	Spire, or tip, on a pagoda.
jaggery	Sugar made from the sap of the toddy palm tree; looks and tastes much like maple sugar.
kalahtino	Chair; or literally, "that on which a foreigner sits."
ka lauk	Wooden elephant bell.
kan	Fate, also "karma."
kaukhnyin	Sticky, salted rice roasted in a section of bamboo.
Kin (masc.)	Title before the given name; indicates royal descent (see *Tin*).
kwé	Dog, usually semi-feral. Also *kwéche* (dirty dog). (See *pi-dog*.)
kyaing	Elephant grass.
kyaung	Monastery (see *Sangha*).
lakh	100,000. Money used in India and Burma.
longyi	Tube-skirt of cloth reaching from waist to ankles, worn by both sexes; men's knotted in front, women's folded in a smooth side-pleat.
maidan	Stage, platform; especially for a *pwé*.
magyi	Burmese name for the tamarind tree.
Maha	Sage, wise one, leader. Maha Muni, a Buddha image

*Indian word

fabled to have been made during the Buddha's lifetime.

*mahaut**	Elephant driver (see *oozie*).
*mahli**	Gardener.
Min Tha	Prince, as in the lead character in a *pwè*, (fem. Min Tha Mi).
mont pyit-salet	Burmese pancake, made of rice flour.
Myothugyi	Head man of a group of five villages, or "circle." Traditionally the villages are related through the mothers.
nagat	Ear stud.
nat	A spirit, often malevolent; also one of thirty-seven officially endorsed spirits who are thought to be disciples of the Buddha, and are often appealed to for favors. Thagyamin is their king.
Né ban	also Neik bam (see *Nirvana*).
Nirvana	State of Oneness with the universal essence (see *Né ban*).
nya yoke-sone	Chili mortar used in the kitchen.
ohn	Coconut. Also *on* (see *gon-bin*).
oozie	Elephant driver. Also *hsin oozie*, (*hsin*, elephant + *oozie*, guide.) Also *mahaut.**
paddy	Unhusked rice, also rice field.
padauk	Burmese rosewood tree. Blooms with clusters of yellow blossoms just before the season of rains.
pah-nat	Thong slipper of reed or wood, usually covered with velvet. Literally, "to be trodden on," also spelled *pha-nat*.
pandal	A temporary structure of bamboo, paper, etc., used as a marquee tent.
Payar	"Lord," "Exalted One." Also used for a pagoda.
Payartaga	Title of respect. One who has built a pagoda.
pongyi	Monk; (literally, "good-great"). One who studies Buddhist scripture. Buddhists do not have priests in the Western sense. Also *phongyi*.

*Indian word

Glossary

pongyi-kyaung	Monastery (see *Sangha*).
Ponna	Brahmin; a Buddhist astrologer.
pwé	Semi-religious "opera."
repoussé	French technique of hammering bas-relief designs into silver. Burmese silversmiths are famous for bowls made in this fashion.
*Salaam**	"Peace be with you," a greeting or farewell. Frequently offered with hands pressed together and head slightly bowed.
salay	Long, white cigar smoked by women and children (see *cheroot*).
Sangha	Buddhist religious order. Brotherhood of Monks.
Saya	Respectful title given to doctors, teachers, astrologers; literally, "learned one."
Sayadaw	Also *Saya Daw*. Prior of a monastery; literally, "head elderly one."
Sayagyi	Learned man, government official, clerk; "big, important."
Shwe Pyidaw	"Golden Land," Burmese name for their country (see *Suvannabhumi*).
shikoe	Prostration, or low bow—the head must touch the floor three times.
sone	A mortar (see *nyayoke-sone*).
Suvanna-bhumi	"Golden Land," Mon name for their kingdom, c. 300 B.C. (see *Shwe Pyidaw*).
thabeit	Alms or begging bowl, usually of black lacquer used by monks.
Thagya-min	King of the nat spirits (see *nat*, also *Thakya Min*).
Thakin	"Lord," term of respect; formerly used toward European bosses.
thanaka	Powder from the padauk tree; cooling astringent.

*Indian word

227

Thugyi	Headman of a village, or group of villages. His/her main task is to reestablish harmony by listening to and arbitrating disputes (see *Myothugyi*).
Tin (fem.)	Title before the given name indicating royal descent. (see *Kin*).
Tripitaka	Buddhist scriptures; literally, "three baskets."
viss	A weight formerly used in Burma and India, equal to about three-and-a-half pounds.
Wun	Magistrate.
yeh oh sin	Water-jar rack.
zawgyi	Sorcerer.
zayat	Rest house.

Bibliography
Sources for the Stories

Babbitt, Ellen C. *The Jatakas: Tales of India.* Appleton Century Crofts, Inc., 1912.

Babbitt, Ellen C. *More Jataka Tales,* Appleton Century Crofts, Inc., 1922.

Brockett, Eleanor. *Burmese and Thai Fairy Tales.* London: Frederick Muller Ltd., 1965. Chicago: Follett, 1967.

Carpenter, Frances; *The Elephant's Bathtub,* New York: Hale/Doubleday 1967.

Cocks, S.W. *Tales and Legends of Ancient Burma.* Bombay: K & J Cooper, (c. 1920; no date given)

Cole, Johanna *Best Loved Folk-tales of the World.* New York: Anchor/ Doubleday, 1983.

DeRoin, Nancy. *Jataka Tales: Fables from the Buddha.* Boston: Houghton Mifflin, 1975.

Htin Aung Maung. *Burmese Folk-Tales.* London: Oxford University Press,1938.

Htin Aung. *Folk Tales of Burma.* New Dehli: Sterling Publishers, 1980.

Klein, Wilhelm. *Burma: Insight Guides.* Hong Kong: Apa Productions Ltd., 1983.

Russell, Maurice. *Told to Burmese Childern.* London: Epworth Press, 1956.

Shway Yoe (Sir James George Scott). *The Burman: His Life and Notions,* 3rd edition. London: Macmillan and Co., Ltd., 1910.

Trager, Helen, and Htin Aung. *A Kingdom Lost for a Drop of Honey.* New York: Parents Magazine Press, 1968.

Troughton, Joanna. *Make Believe Tales and Folk Tales from Burma.* London: Blackie Co., 1951.

Yazawintawkyi, Hmannan. *The Glass Palace Chronicle of the Kings of Burma,* 1829. Translated by Pe Maung Tin and G.H. Luce from Mandalay edition of 1907. First AMS edition, New York: AMS Press Inc., 1976.

Material translated especially for me by Ma May Ngo (Yi) and Than Than Htay, working from material in the Rangoon library.

Recommended Reading

Fiction

⚜ Collis, Maurice. *She Was a Queen.* London: Faber and Faber Ltd. 1937; New York: New Directions, 1991: Fiction, based on information in *The Glass Palace Chronicles,* about events concerning the fall of Pagan in 1257. All ages.

⚜ Garlan, Patricia, and Sunatan, Maryjane. *Orange-Robed Boy.* New York: Viking Press, 1957. A modern story about a twelve-year-old boy who becomes a monk for a short time. This is a traditional custom for most Burmese Buddhist boys. All ages.

⚜ Garlan, Patricia and Sunatan, Maryjane, *The Boy Who Played Tiger.* New York: Viking Press, 1958. All ages. A modern story. Ko Shway is bored and looking for something interesting to do. He is a universal 12-year-old, yet every detail of Burmese village life rings true!

⚜ Gilman, Dorothy. *Incident at Badamyâ.* New York: Fawcett Crest/ Ballantine, 1991. The year is 1950. Imprisoned with six others, Gen, a sixteen-year-old American who has known only Burma as her home, counts on wits, friends and fate to help find her destiny. All ages.

⚜ Lindguist, Willis. *Haji of the Elephants.* New York: McGraw-Hill, 1976. Young Haji uses his knowledge and skill to recapture Majda Koom, a mighty elephant. His life dream to be an *oozie* seems about to come true—until he faces human treachery. All ages.

⚜ Merrill, Jean. *Shan's Lucky Knife.* New York: W.R. Scott, 1950. A retelling of a Burmese folk tale, one of the "Boatman" stories. All ages.

Recommended Reading

Nonfiction

⊀ Aung San Suu Kyi. *Freedom From Fear and Other Writings.* Collected and edited by Michael Aris. New York: Penguin Books, 1995. Some of these inspiring essays are specifically addressed to young people.

⊀ Aung San Suu Kyi. *Letters from Burma.* New York: Penguin Books, 1997. A current look at Burma. Sad yet hopeful.

⊀ Baird-Murray, Maureen. *A World Overturned: A Burmese Childhood.* Northampton, MA: Interlink Publishing, 1998. A captivating autobiography. All ages.

⊀ Cady, John F. *Thailand, Burma, Laos, & Cambodia.* New York: Prentice Hall, 1966. Scholarly and thorough; adult.

⊀ Klein, Wilhelm. Burma: *Insight Guides.* Hong Kong: Apa Productions Ltd. 3rd ed. 1983. A treasure of information; adult.

⊀ Landry, Lionel. *The Land and People of Burma.* New York: Lippincott, 1968. All ages.

⊀ Mannin, Ethel. *Land of the Crested Lion.* London: Jarrolds, 1955. A candid, insightful journey through modern Burma. All ages.

⊀ Seagrave, Gordon S., M.D.. *The Life of a Burma Surgeon.* New York: W. W. Norton & Co., Inc. 1943. All ages.

⊀ Temple, Sir Richard C.. *The 37 Nats.* London: W. Griggs, 1908; republished by Paul Strochan, London: Kiscadale Publications, 1991. Especially valuable for the illustrations. Adult.

Other Titles in the Series

Russian Gypsy Tales
translated by James Riordan • collected by Y. Druts and A. Gessler
ISBN 0-940793-97-0 • $11.95 pb • 160 pages

Imagining Women
Fujian Folk Tales
selected and translated by Karen Gernant
ISBN 1-56656-173-6 • $29.95 hb • ISBN 1-56656-174-4 • $14.95 pb • 288 pages

Tales of the Seal People
Scottish Folk Tales
by Duncan Williamson
Winner of the Anne Izard Storytellers' Choice Award
ISBN 1-56656-101-9 • $24.95 hb • ISBN 1-940793-99-7 • $11.95 pb • 160 pages

The Demon Slayers and Other Stories
Bengali Folk Tales
collected and written by Sayantani DasGupta and Shamita Das Dasgupta
ISBN 1-56656-164-7 • $24.95 hb • ISBN 1-56656-156-6 • $12.95 pb • 224 pages

Children of Wax
African Folk Tales
collected and written by Alexander McCall Smith
ISBN 1-56656-314-3 • $11.95 pb • 128 pages

The Grandfathers Speak
Native American Fok Tales of the Lenapé People
collected and written by Hitakonanulaxk (Tree Beard)
ISBN 1-56656-129-9 • $24.95 hb • ISBN 1-56656-128-0 • $11.95 pb • 160 pages

The Sun Maiden and the Crescent Moon
Siberian Folk Tales
collected and translated by James Riordan
ISBN 0-940793-66-0 • $24.95 hb • ISBN 0-940793-65-2 • $11.95 pb • 224 pages

The Clever Sheikh of the Butana
Sudanese Folk Tales
retold by Ali Lutfi, edited by Kate W. Harris, illustrated by Elnour Hamad
ISBN 01-56656-312-7 • $15.00 pb • 160 pages
